I0613376

Charles Mackay

Luck and What Came of It

Vol. III

Charles Mackay

Luck and What Came of It
Vol. III

ISBN/EAN: 9783743394308

Manufactured in Europe, USA, Canada, Australia, Japa

Cover: Foto ©Andreas Hilbeck / pixelio.de

Manufactured and distributed by brebook publishing software (www.brebook.com)

Charles Mackay

Luck and What Came of It

LUCK;

AND WHAT CAME OF IT.

𝔄 𝔗𝔞𝔩𝔢 𝔬𝔣 𝔬𝔲𝔯 𝔗𝔦𝔪𝔢𝔰.

BY

CHARLES MACKAY.

AUTHOR OF "BARON GRIMBOSH," "UNDER THE BLUE SKY,"
"A MAN'S HEART," ETC., ETC.

VOL. III.

LONDON:
W. H. ALLEN & CO., 13, WATERLOO PLACE,
PALL MALL. S.W.

1881.

(All rights reserved.)

LONDON.
PRINTED BY W. H. ALLEN AND CO., 13 WATERLOO PLACE.

LUCK;

AND WHAT CAME OF IT.

CHAPTER I.

WHILE Lancelot Wyld—after a second tender farewell to Patty Tidy, of which neither his father nor his mother was aware, although his father suspected what might have happened—was speeding his way across the Atlantic, his cousin Herbert was enjoying himself among the studios of the Parisian sculptors, entirely forgetful of his recent journey to Bordeaux and Margaux, and of the unexpected discovery which he and Mr. Octavius Little had made of the supposed heir to the Ravelstone peerage.

III.   1

He was, however, reminded of all the circumstances by a letter from the old lawyer, informing him of Lebrun's sudden disappearance from Swinston, and requesting him to insert an advertisement in " Galignani's Messenger," and in all the journals of Paris and Bordeaux, notifying to the said " Oscar Lebrun, *alias* Oscar D'Autun Lebrun, late of Swinston in the Fens, England," that if he would make known his address to, or communicate with, Mr. Octavius Little, of Swinston aforesaid, or to Mr. Herbert Haughton, Hotel du Louvre, Paris, he would hear of something to his advantage. Herbert duly executed the commission, and waited with curiosity for the results.

Meanwhile, his uncle the Colonel had arrived in Paris, with his friend MacTavish, and invited him to dine at the Café Anglais, where one can have a magnificent repast at a magnificent price, and partake of magnificent wines of the "*premiers crus* " at a price still more magnificent, but never grudged by connoisseurs who can afford to pay it.

It was on the 19th of July 1870 that the three *convives* appointed to meet. Colonel Haughton had invited two old acquaintances, a noted French journalist, who may, for the purpose of this story, be called M. De Nonobstant, and an equally noted banker and financier, who may be called M. Perier Fougard.

The guests assembled in a private cabinet, and did full justice to a *menu* which was the combined production of the genius and experience of Colonel Haughton and M. Fougard—both *gourmets* and *gourmands*—aided by the possibly superior taste and knowledge of the *chef*, who was a *gourmet* only.

The circumstances of the time were peculiar. There had been for a fortnight past a sound as of war trumpets, and an odour as of sulphur and gunpowder, in the intellectual atmosphere of Paris, and all the talk of all the guests was of the immediate declaration of war between France and Prussia.

There was no real ground of warfare or even

1 *

of ill-will between the two countries; for what, if rationally considered, did the occupancy of the Spanish throne by a Prussian Prince signify to the French people?

The nomination of a Hohenzollern to that precarious and dangerous splendour, uninnportant as it ought to have been thought by every sane Frenchman, was considered to be dangerous to the interests of France.

"Prussia to the north of us and Prussia to the south of us is too much," said M. De Nonobstant.

"It may be so," said the banker; "but we shall not be such madmen as to fight about it"

"I think we shall be driven into it," replied the journalist. "The Prussians have never forgotten or forgiven Jena, and all the humiliations they had to suffer at the hands of the First Napoleon, and have meditated revenge for nearly half a century. The French people want the Rhine as a frontier, and the Emperor would only be too happy if he could gratify them,

partly for the sake of the Rhine frontier, partly
for the sake of his dynasty, which he thinks
could never be shaken by the strife of parties,
or by the physical force of revolution, if he
could make the French nation a present of the
coveted territory, and administer to Prussia a
blow that would keep her quiet for half a century
longer."

"I don't believe in the morality of the job, or
that France is strong enough to do it," said
Colonel Haughton, "or that Napoleon the Third
is General enough in himself, or has any other
General under him who is able to accomplish it."

"Nor I either," said MacTavish; "and if
France provokes a war on such a pretence as
this Hohenzollern business, or the supposed
insult to M. Benedetti, she will have the senti-
ment and prejudice of all Europe against her.
If Prussia declares war, well and good; France
must and will fight her, and I think every
patriotic Frenchman will rally to the struggle.
But if France declares war against Prussia, the

strength of Prussia will be doubled and trebled by the sympathy of all Europe."

"Hark! what is that?" said the banker, as the strains of the "Marseillaise" broke in upon them from the Boulevard; and, turning pale as he spoke, he walked hurriedly to the window.

There was a crowd of people marching along the Boulevard with military precision, all singing the patriotic melody in good time, and with contagious enthusiasm.

"There's revolution and civil strife in that infernal tune!" said he. "It is a strain of evil omen; it breeds mischief and disaster. I wonder the police permit it. The very sound of it will send the Funds down two per. cent. to-morrow."

"It's done by authority, and it's a mistake," said De Nonobstant. "The French people can't listen to the 'Marseillaise' with equanimity. It boils their blood, and when the *canaille* hear it, they scent approaching battle, and feel their fingers itch for the plunder of the gunsmiths and the sacking of the Tuileries."

"I like the 'Marseillaise,'" said Herbert Haughton, "and do not wonder that the French are excited by it. What surprises me when I think of it is that the German or Teutonic nations, such as the English, Prussian, Dutch and others, are never moved by a song. They can't feel it. The English haven't a national tune, except 'God save the Queen,' written for the Scotch Jacobites. The most popular tune in England is 'For he's a jolly good fellow,' or 'We won't go home till morning,' a miserable comic thing, borrowed from the French."

"How French?" inquired De Nonobstant. "Can you hum it, or whistle it?"

Herbert hummed it.

"Ah," said M. De Nonobstant, "I see. It is '*Malbrouk s'en va-t-en guerre.*' And is that the most popular of English songs?"

"I am afraid it is," said Colonel MacTavish, who was a Highlander, and had a favourite antipathy to the Sassenach. "The English have no music. I would not give the 'Reel of

Tulloch' for all the music composed or invented
by Englishmen, or any other Sassenachs since
the beginning of the world."

"It affects me grievously," said M. Perier
Fougard, "to hear the 'Marseillaise' in the
streets. I wonder if the Emperor knows of it?
—whether somebody about him has been mad
enough to give the *mot d'ordre* for this pesti-
lential thing to be re-introduced to a public
whom it has driven mad for the best part of a
century?"

"I suspect," said the journalist, pouring out
a glass of choice Richebourg, "that the Emperor—who is not the man he was five years
ago, either in body or in mind—has been over-
persuaded by some sinister female influence to
appeal to the patriotic instincts of the mob by
this song of the Revolution, which has not been
publicly heard in Paris for eighteen years. It
will unloose a flood of ultra-revolutionary and
savage passions, that he and all his armies will
find it difficult to stem. He thinks perhaps it

may help to inflame the war fever. Let him take care that the Commune does not grow out of it and tumble him off his throne."

"The Commune!" said Herbert. "What is the Commune?"

"The Commune," replied M. Perier Fougard, "is organised insanity. It claims to be the only pure Christian doctrine, and asserts that Christ's teaching was that there should be no property except in the Community; that no man should call anything his own but his nose or other parts of his body ; and that, for the sake of his body, it was his duty to work for food to maintain it in health, for raiment to cover it, and for a roof to shelter it; but that all his earnings, over and above the cost of his plainest necessities, should go to the common fund, to provide for him in sickness and old age, and pay for a coffin in which to bury him. The Communists would reduce all men and all women to the rank of bees or emmets ; a hive without lawyers, priests, *gendarmerie*, soldiers, or bankers. I doubt whether it even recognises doctors, and whether the apostles of the movement would not, as the rooks and other creatures do, sentence the infirm to immediate death, as burdens on the public. The Communists consider the Commune to be a religion, and, if need be, they will fight for it as frantically as Christians or Mahometans have ever done for theirs, and will endeavour, if they can, to establish it in the world by fire and sword, and any amount of massacre."

"Just so," observed the journalist. "We Frenchmen know what a burning volcano Communism is. We have seen its lava burst out more than once, and it will burst out again, and will have to be quenched in blood. You English have no idea of the subterranean forces that are at work among the labouring classes of France, the peasantry excepted. We know all about them; and it is the Emperor's best title to his throne, that he has known, as yet, how to repress them."

"But I don't see," said Colonel Haughton, "supposing that all this is true, how it affects the antagonism that exists between Prussia and France."

"But *we* see," said De Nonobstant. "The Emperor knows all about Communism—he was once a Communist, or, at all events, a Socialist himself. He is one of the ablest men of his time; but he is in feeble health, and surrounded by evil counsellors, and wants at one and the same time to stifle Communism, satisfy the Army, and pander to what I must call the wild vainglorious-ness of our people, by a foreign war. And he thinks no war would be so popular as a war against Prussia. It is an old grudge; and, what is more, it is a question of time. If France doesn't declare war against Prussia, Prussia will declare war against France. Who shall be first? that is the problem to be solved."

"Let Prussia be first," said MacTavish, "and place herself in the wrong. 'Thrice is he armed who hath his quarrel just.' He who first in this particular quarrel declares war will be de-feated. See if I am not a true prophet."

The confabulation at this moment was cut short by the shouts of the crowd on the Boulevards, lashed into enthusiasm by the announcement in the evening papers that France had declared war against Prussia. M. Perier Fougard hastily took leave of the party, and descended into the street, and M. De Nonobstant accompanied him, leaving the Englishmen to themselves.

The news was true. The frenzy of the crowd was marvellous. The "Marseillaise" was shouted by thousands of men, women, and children, as well as by the hoarse throats of the riff-raff and the scoundrelism that always fester in great cities, the boils and sores of the body politic. And amid the pauses of the sublime hymn—sublime even in the untutored voices of the multitude—arose the shrill cry of the "gutter children," "To Berlin! to Berlin!"

Paris had gone mad, and had not been so mad since 1849, twenty-one years previously, during which interval its insanity, owing to the energy of one man and his legions, had been imprisoned in a straight waistcoat, and that man, that very day, had staked his throne, his dynasty, his life, on a forlorn hope. Alas!

The three Englishmen took a stroll on the Boulevards, critical, each of them, of the seething frenzy of the mob. Colonel MacTavish, a real soldier of the battlefields (not like Colonel Haughton, a mere soldier of the clubs), and a very cannie Scotsman, to boot, and who weighed and pondered everything, and wrought out his conclusions from facts, or what he supposed to be facts—was of opinion that the Emperor was mad, and that the French people were madder still. He thought, moreover, that the French army was a paper army, and not an army of bones and blood; and that the clash between Prussia and France would be like the clash and crash of cast iron with crockery and porcelain. But his companions laughed him to scorn. The war notes of the " Marseillaise " sounded in their ears; the shouts of the ever-surging and boiling multitude, that seemed to proclaim the settled purpose of a great nation, impressed them differently, and they felt that had they been Frenchmen, they too, like the mob of the streets, might have joined in the cry, " To Berlin ! " irrational as it was.

Chance, not design, directed their steps towards the Grand Opera. They entered. The opera in course of performance—and half concluded, before they took, not their seats, but such standing room as they could find—was Auber's magnificent " Muette de Portici," known to the Italian stage as " Masaniello," a very dangerous piece to represent in times of revolutionary excitement. When the curtain fell, at the close of the third act, there was a cry that seemed to be spontaneous and unpremeditated from all parts of the house, " The Marseillaise ! The Marseillaise ! " An actress stepped forward, a Madame Marie Sasse, and commenced to sing it with a clear ringing voice, when somebody in the boxes, who was evidently well-known to the audience, shouted out "*Debout! Debout!*" " Stand up! Stand up." The audience rose as one man, and joining in the chorus, made the rafters ring with the reverberations of the magnificent anthem. So great was the excitement that many women fainted and many strong men wept.

"A queer folk, the French," said Colonel MacTavish.

"Fools," said Colonel Haughton.

"Heroes," said Herbert Haughton.

When the friends parted, the latter went to his hotel alone. On his arrival he found a letter from England awaiting him. It was in a handwriting with which he was unacquainted, and ran thus:—

Honord Sir,

Me and my wyf is in grate distress, and has been for sum time—ever sins you went away, and never wanted her to stand as a moddal. If you woud kindly lett Arabella have five pounds, as a lone, it will save us from grate sufferin. Being her husban I don't like her to

stand as a moddal, but if you have enny statute
as you 've began, and cant do without her, I
don't mind to lett her stand a few times, at a
sovraign a time. Waitin your anser, I am,
honored Sir, your humble servant,

                              JOSEPH GRIGG.
Mr. Haughton, Esq.

Herbert read and re-read the epistle. He was
stunned. He was chagrined. He was indignant.
"What!" he thought, "the beautiful Arabella,
the perfection of form, the beau ideal of female
loveliness—Arabella, with the limbs of a goddess,
every contour of whose mortal frame is moulded
as if it were to be a pattern of the divine ideal of
what humanity is capable of becoming at its very
best and highest—married! and married to a
fellow named Grigg, a tailor perhaps, or a dust-
man, or a costermonger!" He had thought sometimes, as the reader is aware, that he could have
married her himself, in spite of the world and all
its opinions and prejudices, in spite of his father,

mother, sisters, and all his kin, near or remote, if he could have called such a treasure of divine beauty his own, and his only. And to think that this transcendent creature had thrown herself away upon a costermonger! He did not know that Grigg was a costermonger, but it gave him a ferocious and unreasonable delight, very much akin to a pain or a torment, to think that he was. Arabella Grigg! Faugh! What a name for one fairer and more shapely than Aphrodite. The fellow, if not a costermonger or such like, was probably some boosy mechanic who, in a drunken fit some day, might kick her to death with his heavy boots, and mar Nature's choicest work by his brutality.

"What a horrid world," he thought to himself, "is this, that I live in! And yet, after all, if she were fool enough to marry this coster-monger, or this boosy shoemaker, or whatever else he may be, haven't I had a lucky escape? Oughtn't I to be glad that she has not fallen to my lot? What should I have done with her if I had got her? To love a woman for her form! Bah! Form deteriorates. What would the lovely Arabella be in ten years? She would be fat, frowsy, dowdy, and without a mind; while I with the same ideas of beauty that I have now— but more educated and refined and exactive perhaps of impossible conditions from my stupid Venus—would hate her; and then what would become of me? I've had a lucky escape. That she should have married a costermonger, how I hate the villain!—is a proof that she never could have suited me. I rather like her for finding her level. No, I don't; I hate the creature! She shall never sit or stand to me again, and I will finish my Aphrodite without her. But all the same, she was a beautiful specimen of a young woman, and I ought, perhaps, to be grateful that I ever had the chance of studying her magnificence. But Arabella Grigg! Ah me! It is too bad, and it darkens the sunshine in my sky."

Mr. Herbert Haughton took this matter very

much to heart, although he reasoned upon it much after the fashion of the fox with the grapes in Æsop's immortal story. The sentimental side of his character was wounded. But the practical side was not hurt. On the contrary, it was comforted. The fact became apparent to himself, and that was a victory. He had never been in love. His fancy had been captivated; that was all. And the fancy was dead, and would speedily be buried and forgotten. *Vive la bagatelle!* And with these reflections Herbert Haughton went to bed, and did not sleep much the worse for the weight of them.

Next morning, on reconsidering the matter, the fair form of Arabella seemed to float continually before his eyes—Arabella without the Grigg, Arabella without the garments, the fairest sight to his artistic eyes that creation afforded. To the Arabella of his fancy, a thousand pounds would have been a small sum to advance, if he had it; but to Arabella with the Grigg attached, five pounds was a large one. Nevertheless, he

2 *

resolved to send it to her, if she were really Mrs. Grigg, and Grigg no impostor. He discovered in due time that Grigg had told a true story. He accordingly sent him the money.

———————

CHAPTER II.

EVENTS in France marched rapidly. The war absorbed all men's thoughts, and the episode of the " Divine Arabella," who was so much more human than he had imagined, determined Mr. Herbert Haughton, disgusted for a while with his London studies, to remain a little longer in Paris, to be a spectator of scenes that were likely to become historical.

His uncle the Colonel, for reasons of his own, partly gastronomical, partly curious as to the progress of the war, resolved to imitate his example; and Colonel MacTavish, having come out for a holiday, thought it better to enjoy it in

Paris than anywhere else, especially as he might
gratify his military instincts by criticising the
war into which the Emperor had rushed so im-
petuously and, as he thought, so unwisely, and
studying the temper of the French people, either
in the success or the failure which would result
from the Emperor's onset.

He had heard of the search for Oscar Lebrun,
and took so much of an idle man's interest in
what did not concern him, as to feel a vague kind
of curiosity to know what would come of it.
Heirs to peerages and fortunes were, as he re-
flected, not hunted for every day, and there might
be sport, or at least a little languid excitement,
in watching the progress of the adventure.

But Oscar Lebrun entered no appearance,
either personally or by letter, and Herbert
Haughton, after the lapse of a fortnight, thought
it advisable to repeat his advertisement, and to
order its insertion daily in all the newspapers of
Paris and Bordeaux.

He had not to wait above ten days longer to

receive the tidings he expected. At the end of
that time, when all Paris was ringing with the
questionable news that daily reached the Empress
and her ministers from the German frontier—
news that was carefully sifted before it was
permitted to reach the public ears; news that,
when hopelessly bad, was made to appear, for
half an hour at the utmost, to be hopefully good
—he received a card from the *concièrge*, on which
was inscribed, in manuscript, "Oscar D'Autun
Lebrun."

Herbert's heart, as he afterwards said, went
"pit-a-pat" at the announcement, and it took
him some minutes to collect his thoughts, and
to put on that air of indifference which he wished
to assume, but was far from feeling.

He descended into the waiting-room, and found
a young man of prepossessing appearance, with
dark hair, fresh-coloured face, tall, aristocratic
looking, scrupulously well dressed, wearing a
moustache but no beard, with an open, intellectual countenance, entirely self-possessed,

and with all the polished manners of a gentleman.

"Do you speak English?" said Herbert
Haughton.

"I do, tolerably well," replied Oscar. "I am
half an Englishman."

"Would you object to come with me to my
bed-room? The business on which I have summoned you is both important and delicate, and
it would be well if we could discuss it pri-
vately."

"By all means," said Oscar.

And Herbert led the way. As soon as both
were seated he went straight to the business in
hand, detailed his and Mr. Little's adventures in
Margaux in search of the descendants, if any
there were, of Arthur Haughton, an officer in
the British Naval Service, who had married in
France, and been wholly lost sight of by his
English relatives.

"I am the grandson of that Englishman," said
Oscar; "but I learn from your lips for the first

time that he had any known relatives in England.
I never made any inquiry, neither, as far as I
know, did my father. My grandfather I never
saw."

"But, the case being so, and knowing that
your grandfather's name, and your father's, and
your own, was Haughton, will you permit me to
ask why it was changed to Lebrun?"

"I cannot tell; but I believe my grandfather
took my grandmother's name for the love he
bore her, and possibly to obliterate the traces of
his English nationality."

"But why should he do so?"

"I cannot answer. Perhaps he loved France
better than England; perhaps it was a whim, a
caprice ; I know not. Perhaps my father, being
a Frenchman born, and never having been in
England, did not appreciate the ugly English
consonants in the name, which a Frenchman
would be likely to mispronounce. The D'Autun
in my name represents Haughton, I suppose,
though I never thought of it before. But will

you tell me why you have sent for me, and if you are related to Mr. Archibald Haughton of Swinston?"

"I am his only son."

"And the brother of Euphemia Haughton?"

Oscar's heart beat violently as he put the question. He felt the warm blood rushing to his cheeks, and his eyes sparkled with more than their wonted fire.

"The same," replied Herbert; "and I have sent for you to inform you that, if you are the grandson of Lieutenant Haughton, you are the heir to the English peerage of Ravelstone and a hundred thousand pounds!"

"And Euphemia is my cousin! *Mon Dieu! mon Dieu!*" he added, lapsing into French. "*La nouvelle m'accable de joie!*"

"And do you think so very much of a peerage that you express such joy?" asked Herbert, who would have had no objection himself to the said peerage in reversion.

"I despise a peerage!" replied Oscar, em-

phatically. "I am a Republican *de pur sang,*
and think that hereditary rank and title is a relic
of barbarism. I am for fraternity and equality,
as well as for liberty; and I glory in being a
workman, able to gain my own honest bread by
my own honest labour. If I am an English
peer, I will never assume the title, but be plain
Oscar Lebrun to the end of my days. But
I bless the peerage, nevertheless, and feel
afraid of my own good fortune. *La joie fait
peur!*"

"You speak in riddles, Mr. Lebrun," said
Herbert. "You despise a peerage, and yet you
bless it!"

"I despise it as a barbarism; but I bless it
because it may be the means of giving me that
which is worth ten thousand peerages and all
the wealth in the world—the possession of the
woman I love, fairer than Venus, purer than
Diana! A great impediment stood between us.
If I am the heir to an English peerage, the
impediment is removed."

Herbert thought that Oscar, his cousin, as he believed he must be, was a very superior young man, to have passed his life among journeymen mechanics, yet to have ideas like these and to express them in such choice phraseology. Oscar continued,

"Mr. Haughton, can you tell me who would have been the next heir to this peerage in default of me and my claims?"

"My father," answered Herbert, "and after my father, myself."

"*Ne m'en voulez pas!* Don't blame me if I have innocently deprived you of the heritage you might have expected. I would give it up to you with all my heart, renounce it in your favour, renounce it and all that belongs to it, with a gladsome heart, if only for the removal of the obstacle that stood between me and my heart's best treasure."

"The renunciation is impossible, Mr. Lebrun; but since you have taken me into your confidence and entrusted me with the secret of your heart, may I ask you if chance or design first led you into my father's service?"

"Chance entirely, and a chance that is extraordinary to reflect upon, that brought me among my kindred without my knowledge."

"And secondly, may I ask if she who may possibly become the future Lady Ravelstone knows of your good fortune ?"

"How can she ?" answered Oscar, "unless you have told her. If I knew nothing until this hour, how can *she* have known ?"

"But how can *I* have told her ? I do not know her."

"You *do* know her. She is your sister Euphemia, Mr. Haughton."

Herbert started.

"Why, it's a positive romance, Mr. Lebrun, and if it were introduced into a novel, everybody would say the whole thing was most improbable, if not impossible."

"The improbable is much more commonly true than people imagine."

"But what was the great obstacle in your path, Mr. Lebrun, if my sister loved you and you loved her? "

" Your father, an employer of many workmen, paying me weekly wage, and likely, in my opinion—though I may have done him wrong—to have opposed the union of his daughter with a person so far beneath the social position of an employer as one of his workmen. Your father never condescended to exchange a word with me, except on his business, and seemed to think that I was of no more account, socially considered, than his horse or his ox."

" You do my father wrong," replied Herbert, warmly. " He is as much of a democrat as you are, and a man altogether above prejudice. He hasn't an atom of false pride."

" Perhaps not, by nature ; but in England class amounts to caste, and a wider gulf separates an English capitalist from his labourer than that which separates a Brahmin from a pariah. The English employer, as a rule, thinks no more

of his people than he does of the wheels and cogs
of his machinery; and the English workman, on
his part, thinks his employer a hard and selfish
tyrant, whom it would be a pleasure to discomfit,
if not to plunder, and suspects any kindness
which he may chance to offer to be a snare and
a treachery."

"I cannot discuss the question. I have no knowledge ; but I hope you're wrong. If you are
right, what is to be the future of England? "

" Stern Revolution! " replied Oscar. " What
do you think would have been the position
of England at this day, if Christopher Co-
lumbus, four centuries ago, had not discovered
America ? If the discontented spirits of Great
Britain, deprived of land, without the remotest
chance of procuring any, to cultivate for their
daily needs, had not had the opportunity of
owning land in the New World, what would your
great landed proprietors have been worth in the
present day ? Where would have been your
Dukes of Westminster, and Bedford, and Buc-

cleugh, and Sutherland, and all the rest of them, if the expatriated millions had remained at home to compete with them on their narrow soil for broad acres to grow bread upon? Their lands would have known them no more, but would have been divided among the sovereign people, who alone give land a commercial value."

" There are no lands," said Herbert, " attached to the Ravelstone peerage, and if you are Lord Ravelstone, and take your seat in the House of Lords, and give utterance to opinions such as you have just expressed, you will create a very unpleasant sensation. An ultra-Republican—not to say a Communist—Peer would be a novelty."

" I shall not sit in the House of Lords. I don't want the title; I won't have it. I will claim it, if it be mine, for the sake of my love, and then drop it for ever, as something unworthy of the principles which I have adopted, and which I have sworn to defend with my honour and my life."

" Sworn to defend with your honour and your
life! and you an expectant bridegroom! I can
only say that if I were a woman, and you my
suitor, I would not accept you as long as you
entertained such ideas."

It struck Oscar very suddenly and forcibly
that his two characters of ardent lover and
zealous world-reformer were not very much in
harmony, and that Mr. Herbert Haughton was
drawing him into a corner of argument, where
it would not be very convenient for him to be
placed at the moment when the news of his good
fortune was so fresh upon him.

He therefore felt relieved when Herbert,
noticing the sombre and uneasy expression that
passed over Oscar's countenance, changed the
subject, and asked him when he intended to go
to Swinston and confer with Mr. Little, to learn
from that high authority the truth of his altered
position, and the duties incumbent upon him in
consequence?

This was a new perplexity to Oscar. His

III.   3

first impulse was to start for England on the morrow morning, to see Euphemia, and afterwards her father and mother, and to formally make her an offer of his hand, his fortune, and his life. His next was to confer with the redoubtable "Maireann," in which case he would either have to retire from the Confederacy, under such penalties as it might choose to inflict for his recusancy, or to be bound anew to its allegiance, "soul and body, heart and brain," and the sacrifice of every other interest in life, actual or prospective. The dilemma was grave, and its contemplation filled him with alarm.

"All for love, or the world well lost," was a familiar saying; but was he to forego the holy cause of the "Maireann," of Equality, of Fraternity, and of the Commune, even for the sake of love, great, divine and holy as love was ? He longed for solitude, that he might confer with his own soul on this momentous question, and suddenly brought the colloquy to a close.

"This news, Mr. Haughton," he said, "has

come very suddenly upon me. I know not to-day what I shall decide to-morrow. I have given you my confidence. I know you will respect it. I shall be glad to see you again if I remain in Paris, or if I go to England."

"I hope so," said Herbert; "but meanwhile, my uncle, Colonel Haughton, my father's brother, is in Paris. Let me introduce you to him. Come and dine with us to-morrow at the Café Anglais—say at seven?"

"I will come," replied Oscar, glad to be relieved, even for a few hours, of the embarrassment of further discussion with his kinsman.

Oscar returned to his solitary lodgings in the Rue Taranne, and indited a letter to Mr. Archibald Haughton, describing his interview with his son Herbert, and avowing his love for his daughter Euphemia. He also informed Mr. Little that he had seen his advertisement, and that as soon as he could arrange some small affairs in Paris he would wait upon him at Swinston.

3 *

There yet remained a third letter, the most important of all, a letter to Euphemia herself, setting forth with all the ardour of youthful passion the blissful change in his fortunes and in his very personality, that had turned the twilight of his fears and hopes into the full noontide of a perfect day, and enabled him to meet her father as man to man, equal to equal, king to king—and only a king that she might become his queen.

He wrote yet another letter to his colleagues in the " Maireann," announcing his departure from Paris; but on reading it over before sealing it up, he thought that one thing at a time was enough to occupy him, that this time was the time for his love and for his love only, and that the great question of the regeneration of the working classes might await his leisure.

He placed the letter on the hearth and set fire to it. He watched the flames consume it, and, as it was gradually reduced to ashes, felt relieved of a weight of anxiety, and finally resolved to leave Paris on the morrow after the dinner at which he had promised to meet Herbert and Colonel Haughton, the newly-found relatives, in whose estimation he desired to stand well, not exactly for their sakes, but for the sake of her who had been dear to his heart in the days of his lowly estate, but who was dearer still in this day, when no pride of birth or station could throw its dark shadow between them.

CHAPTER III.

IT was on the 6th of August, seventeen days after the declaration of war, that Herbert Haughton escorted Oscar Lebrun to the Café Anglais, to dine with Colonels Haughton and MacTavish.

They were all very favourably impressed by his appearance, manners, and conversation, and thought that the newly-found heir to the family honours of the Haughtons deserved his good fortune.

Oscar was full of anxiety relative to the progress of the war. News had arrived in the morning of the defeat and death of General Douay on the previous day at Wissembourg, and sinister rumours circulated on the Boulevards, of greater and more recent calamities that had befallen the French arms.

Oscar excused himself from a long sitting at the table, on the plea that he was a dull companion, in view of the preoccupation of his mind, as well as a pre-engagement.

Colonel Haughton, whose aristocratic prejudices had been sorely wounded by the bare idea that a working man, a mechanic, could possibly be transformed into a peer, was agreeably surprised to find that the working man was a gentleman. His family pride had been rudely shocked when he learned that his elder brother, as he not very elegantly phrased it, " had had his nose put out of joint " by an obscure interloper, of whose previous existence nobody was aware; but being a practical man, he came to the conclusion that it was not only wise to make the best of things, but that in this particular case the best was very good, and that the newly-found heir, whatever he might have been previously by circumstance,

was by nature quite as good a Haughton as himself, or his brother, and worthy to wear the
honours that had descended to him.

"It is in the blood, you see," he remarked to
Colonel MacTavish, with a gracious nod to Herbert. "The true blue blood always tells."

"Not so sure about blue blood," said Mac-
Tavish. "I like red blood best. Blood improves,
and blood deteriorates. I don't believe in hard and
fast lines in blood or anything else. May not the
son of an ignorant boor, if he be produced and
born under a kindly conglomeration of—well,
what shall I say? but you know what I mean—
become as great a gentleman, fate and circumstance favouring, as the son of a Duke? Adam
delved, and Eve span; and all the big wigs and
great gentlemen in the world proceeded, we are
told, from that pair."

"Some philosophers doubt that," said Colonel
Haughton. "But I won't go into that question. Nevertheless, I maintain that blood tells."

"What *is* blood?" persisted MacTavish. One

of the greatest blackguards I know is a member
of one of the noblest and most ancient families
of England. What has blood done for him, I
should like to know. The footman who stands
behind his chair is an honester fellow than he,
is better behaved, and better looking. Is there
no blood, worthy to be so called, in anybody's
veins, unless his ancestors have been beknighted,
or be-baronetted, or be-lorded, a century or two
before his birth? Bah! I think your newly-
found relative is one that you ought to be proud
of. Nature has done much for him, and education has carried on Nature's good work. His new
position has given him no new dignity, it has
only enabled us all to notice in him what we
never should have noticed had he continued in
his previous condition of life, and presented
himself before us with grimy hands, and a blouse
on."

"Doubtless," replied Colonel Haughton.
"You know what Napoleon the First remarked
when a too slavish flatterer asserted that he had

an angelic smile. 'I had the same smile when I was a poor sub-lieutenant, but nobody saw anything heavenly in it at that time.'"

"Of course not," said MacTavish; "a smile is of no account, and is not heavenly at all if the smiler has nothing to give away; in a woman's case, her favour, and in a man's or an Emperor's or a King's, money, place, pension, dignity, and all the rest of it. A smile with no advantage behind it, is no smile at all, only a grimace."

Herbert Haughton had not, up to this time, had an opportunity of informing his uncle of the fact that Oscar, while in his father's employ, and wholly unconscious of his relationship to that gentleman, had become enamoured of his sister Euphemia, and that the latter, as far as he could understand, looked favourably upon his suit.

Colonel Haughton received the information without expressing, and perhaps without feeling surprise.

"It's certainly singular, if not romantic," he

said, "and seems to me to be a very fortunate arrangement for all parties. How does your father like the idea?"

"I have not heard. I have not been home since the discovery of Mr. Oscar's identity; but I don't suppose either my father or my mother will object, unless there is something against the young man's character, which, from appearances, I do not think is likely."

"What a sensation it will make in that miserable little hole, Swinston," said Colonel Haughton. "Why the very stones of the High Street, and all the little side streets and alleys will gabble about it."

"Yes," said the other Colonel; "and how the local papers will print columns of rubbish about it! If the pair ever marry, as I think they will, I hope that they'll be married in London, if only to deprive the stupid, idle, chattering donkeys of that most horrible of all howling wildernesses, an English country town, of an opportunity to get drunk."

"Well," said Colonel Haughton, "the poor clodhoppers of Swinston would be much the better of a stone thrown into the stagnant pool of their daily lives! Besides, who in London would care for the marriage of Lord Ravelstone with his fair cousin—say at St. Georges, Hanover Square—except the nursery maids, the cooks (if there be a woman cook worthy of the name left in this miserable world), and all the tawdry draggle-tailed hussies of the neighbourhood? Whereas, down at Swinston it would be a tempest in a slop basin. There would be triumphal arches, and bands of music, and ringing of bells, and the distribution of beer and coals to an ungrateful multitude, and the firing of guns, and perhaps an ox roasted whole."

"Horrible barbarism!" said MacTavish; "worthy only of cannibals. Did you ever taste a slice from an ox roasted whole?"

"Never," said Colonel Haughton, with an expression of intense disgust. "A cut from an ox roasted whole might suit a hungry and un-

critical dog, or, as you say, a cannibal, but not a
Christian, or a gentleman."

On retiring after dinner to one of the great
cafés on the Boulevards, instead of spending
the evening at one of the theatres, the three
Englishmen found the crowd no longer seated
at the little tables playing the eternal game of
dominoes and drinking the abominable absinthe,
the Frenchman's delight, but gathered together
in groups, gesticulating fiercely, and all speaking
at the same time. It was a veritable Babel and
confusion of tongues, although all the speakers
spoke the same language.

Colonel Haughton noticed in the crowd, in the
midst of a group to which he was holding forth,
his friend M. Perier Fougard, the banker, and
attracting his attention as speedily as he could,
asked him in French what was the matter.

"The matter is," said the banker, in English,
"that bad news, the worst possible news, has
arrived; that the accursed Prussians—the Huns,
the Vandals, the Pandours!—are carrying all

before them, and that we may have them in
Paris in less than a fortnight!"

"You don't say so!" replied the Colonel,
using the very stupid conventional phrase which
Englishmen employ when they are much surprised or slightly incredulous, though they know
very well that the person they address does state
the very thing, which they say he does *not* state.

At this moment Oscar Lebrun entered the
café, and catching sight of the Englishmen, went
straight up to them. He asked eagerly, if not
abruptly, if they had heard that the Emperor
had lost a great battle. They had not heard
the particulars, and could scarcely credit the
intelligence.

"Ill news travels fast," said Oscar, in English. "You will, I think, discover by to-morrow
that it is true. The Emperor, deceived by
others, deceived himself, and thought to crumple
up Prussia like a strong man crumples up a
sheet of paper; but he is likely to be crumpled
up himself."

"But will the people not rally around him if fortune seems to go against him?" asked Colonel Haughton. "The people drove the Emperor into war against his better judgment, and they ought to stand by him all the faster because he has lost a battle."

"But they won't!" said Oscar. "Men who play such high games as his, must succeed and get small credit, or fail and be doomed to perdition. The Emperor's throne will not be worth sixpence unless he gain a victory that shall make amends for the present loss. The Republic —not the three-coloured one but the red one— will be proclaimed in less than twenty-four hours after the Emperor loses a great battle. It was my intention to start for England to-night and become an Englishman. But I am a Frenchman now, and will not desert my country. *Vive la France!*"

"And my sister?" whispered Herbert, unheard of the Colonels.

Oscar, whose face had previously been flushed

with excitement, turned somewhat pale. He took Herbert's hand and pressed it firmly.

"My heart is hers, my arm is my country's!"

"Take my advice," replied Herbert, "and go to England as you first intended. You can do no good here. You are a Frenchman no longer. Let us go together while there is time. If the Prussians win—as they seem likely to do—what then?"

"What then? Why, every Frenchman's arm will be needed, and mine among the rest."

"Excuse me if I seem to dictate, or even to offer advice; but I think, under the private circumstances in which you are placed, you owe it to yourself, as well as to my father, to go to England, and establish your identity to the satisfaction of all the Haughtons, and of their lawyer, Mr. Little. I do not think you have any right to let the matter rest in abeyance, or in doubt; for there is a doubt, until you make doubt impossible by the production of the legal papers that establish your birth and parentage.

It is just possible, also, that if you stay many
days longer in Paris, you may be unable to get
out of it, however ardently you may desire to do
so. I shall leave to-morrow."

Oscar meditated; but it was for a few moments
only. After all, he was only partially a Frenchman. He was of English blood; he had English
interests which transcended all that he had in
France; and the sweet face of Euphemia Haughton was a magnet that drew him towards her
with all but irresistible force, and compelled him
to forget his patriotism—if he were indeed a
patriot, of which he was not entirely sure—and
to remember only that he was a lover, and a
happy one.

He was, moreover, convinced by Herbert's
representations, and glad to have the support of
reason and social duty for taking the course into
which love alone would have been sufficient to
impel him.

So the difficulty was solved. The two young
men announced their determination to Colonel

Haughton and his friend MacTavish. They were both surprised at the suddenness of the movement; but Colonel Haughton made no objection; how could he?

"Tell my brother," he said, "that I shall remain in Paris a week or two longer. This is a great historical time, and I want to see, on the spot, the fate of the Buonapartes."

Next morning Oscar and Herbert started by the first train for Boulogne and Folkestone, and learned on the way to understand each other more intimately than they had done previously.

CHAPTER IV.

On arriving at Charing Cross, the young men took leave of each other, Herbert repairing to his studio—not without a passing thought of the "divine Arabella," that lost Pleiad, fallen from the poetical heaven in which his imagination had placed her, into the miry prose of matrimony with a costermonger—and Oscar to the Great Northern Hotel, to be ready for a journey to the Fens by the earliest train.

Although he knew that Mr. Haughton and his family were still in London, and although it would have given him heartfelt joy and satis-

4 *

faction to catch a glimpse even of the robe of his
beloved, if the felicity of seeing her face was not to
be allowed him, he thought that his first business
was to present himself at the office of Mr. Little
of Swinston, and exhibit for the perusal of that
gentleman the credentials that supported his
claim to be the grandson of his grandfather.

He had all the documents in his pocket-book,
and had preserved them for years; and though
he had often examined them, had never suspected
that his grandfather's name of D'Autun had been
changed from Haughton, or given the matter a
thought when in Mr. Haughton's employ.

At what time his grandfather had assumed the
name of Lebrun in addition to that of D'Autun
he did not know; but he judged, as Mr. Little
had conducted an inquiry into the matter on the
spot that that gentleman might be better informed
than himself.

Mr. Little received him with great courtesy
and kindness, for the lawyer was thoroughly
persuaded in his own mind that Oscar was, *de*

jure and *de facto*, Lord Ravelstone, a peer of the realm, a comparatively rich man, and altogether an important personage; but he would not call him " My Lord" just yet, for it was his business as an experienced practitioner not to appear too sure of anything, or any person, until doubt had been rendered impossible.

Begging Oscar to be seated, he read all his documents with careful scrutiny, Oscar all the while watching every change in the expression of his face.

"I am afraid," he said at last, "that this business is not so simple as it looks. Arthur Haughton seems, for reasons of his own, to have Gallicised his name into D'Autun. It is an unsafe thing, though perfectly legal—at least it is in England—for a man to change his name, either for good reasons or bad ones. It leads to difficulty and expense, and suggests inquiries where none would otherwise have been necessary. In this case, however troublesome it may be, we have to prove that D'Autun was Haugh-

ton.   Then your grandfather, for such I must
believe he was, rendered confusion worse confounded by adding Lebrun to a changed name,
which brings on the question, whether there may
not have been three different persons,—mind, I
don't say there were, but there *may* have been—
in Margaux at the very time when your grandfather lived and married there;—three separate
persons—Haughton, D'Autun, and Lebrun.
Now we have to make it legally manifest that
these possibly three persons were, in reality, one."

"No doubt," said Oscar ; "and it will not be
difficult.   Another inquiry on the spot, armed
with all the powers of law to examine witnesses
and test evidence, will put the matter right, and
will not, I suppose, be very expensive."

"Law, my Lord—I mean Mr. Lebrun—is a
very costly commodity.   But as this investigation will be a friendly one, for the only persons
who might suppose themselves interested in
opposing you are Mr. Archibald Haughton and
his son Herbert, and as they will not oppose but

aid the investigation, I do not see that the cost of the inquiries will be very heavy. It is for you to do the rest and complete all the links in the chain of your identity."

"Will you undertake the task for me professionally?"

"Mr. Haughton is my client, and should your position and his become antagonistic, I could not act for both. Not that I anticipate antagonism; but still, I advise you to complete your case by your own solicitor or *avocat* in Bordeaux; and you will forgive me for adding that you should lose no time about it."

"I thank you," replied Oscar. "And will you pardon me if I ask you—not as a client seeking legal advice, but as a young man appealing to one older—whether, under all the circumstances, I ought to present myself before Mr. Haughton? I have special and sacred reasons for desiring to do so without delay."

The lawyer, who was not in the secret of Oscar's affections, was puzzled.

" Without being aware of your special reasons," he said at last, " I cannot well advise
you, though I think that, if I were in your
place, and there were no overpowering hurry or
necessity, I should postpone seeking an interview
with him until I could meet him as Lord Ravelstone, in clear and indisputable possession of the
title."

Oscar sighed. " That might take a week or
ten days," he said ; " and meantime I am
miserable."

" That 's not a long time ! " replied Mr. Little.
" But, as far as I am concerned, you talk riddles,
so that all I say, in my ignorance of the facts,
must go for nothing."

Oscar, like other people who ask advice that
is not given in accordance with their own pre-
conceived ideas of what the advice ought to be,
resolved to take his own course, and begged the
lawyer's pardon for having troubled him.

" Shall I leave my papers with you ? " he
asked.

"Well, you may," replied Mr. Little, "and I will communicate their contents to Mr. Haughton, as the next heir to the Ravelstone peerage in your default, and who, before he recognises you as the true heir, ought to be fully satisfied."

"I wish to Heaven," said Oscar, in a burst of fervour, "that Mr. Haughton were the true heir. A peerage will be of no use to me. I don't want it. I shan't prize it. It will sit awkwardly upon me. All I want is the hand of Euphemia Haughton;—her heart I believe is mine. With her my own, all the peerages in the world might go begging for me, before I would accept the grandest of them all at the price of relinquishing her."

"Hallo!" said Little. "Is that the state of the case, young man—that is, my Lord?"

"I believe it is," replied Oscar. "I loved Miss Euphemia when there seemed to be an insuperable barrier of social position and prejudice between us, and I blessed the peerage when

I heard of it, because it removed that barrier. Otherwise I don't care about it. I would gladly be plain Oscar Lebrun to the end of my days, and leave the peerage to Mr. Haughton, and all the money attendant upon it, on the sole condition that he would bless my union with his daughter!"

"That is out of a lawyer's line altogether," replied Mr. Little; "and I can say no more in the matter than to express my earnest hope that the lady may be yours, and excuse me if I add, that I think you deserve her."

"Thank you," said Oscar, his eyes flashing with pleasure. "You understand me better than you did when I first entered the room, and I think I understand you better also. I shall not hesitate to present myself before Mr. Haughton as soon as I reach London, and tell him face to face, and man to man, what I have told you."

Oscar's change of fortune had become known to all Swinston;—too small a town for a secret. Neither Mr. Haughton nor his family had

breathed a word of it, nor had Mr. Little, or any
of his people; but things do become known in a
very mysterious manner in little communities,
and spread from mouth to mouth with electric
rapidity.

Mrs. Stebbings was among the first to hear
that her old lodger had been advertised for, and
discovered to be the heir to a peerage, and a
large fortune; and the big news so troubled her
small mind that she was positively unhapy
until she had communicated the information not
only to her husband and daughters, but to the
butcher's wife, and the baker's wife, and the
greengrocer's wife, and the carpenter's wife, and
the tailor's wife, and the shoemaker's wife, and
to every woman in the town with whom she was
on speaking terms.

" Lord love you! " said Mrs. Stebbings to Mrs.
Smith, the tailor's wife, her next-door neighbour,
" I always know'd as he wasn't a Frenchman.
How could he be, when he could speak English
as well as you or me, Mrs. Smith? A French-

man is always dirty, and he was as clean as a
new pin, and quite regular and proper; and then
he played the pianner better than old Jones
plays the organ, and sung as well as the men in
the theayter that I wunst heard when I was in
London. He wasn't a working man! Not he!
He only purtended, in order that he might be
near a certain young woman! You know who
who I mean. But the artfulness of it, if he
knew all the while that he was that young
woman's cousin, and head of the family!"

"But," said Mrs. Smith, "suppose he didn't
know! He wasn't the head of the family afore
Lord Ravelstone and his son were drownded;
and, as far as I can see, hadn't any right to
expect that ever he would be, supposing always
that he knew his real name to be Haughton,
and not Lebrun."

"I can't argufy about it," replied Mrs. Stebbings; "but it's my belief that the young gentleman—for he is a gentleman, and no mistake—
is awful sly, and that he knew all along who was

who, and what was what; and all the while he
stayed with me he never took no notice of my
daughter Matilda, as pretty a girl you know,
Mrs. Smith, as ever set foot on the streets of
Swinston, and who was as good as him any day,
if he were only a workman, and her the daughter
of a respectable tradesman. He know'd he was
a Lord all along. I 'm certain he did."

Mrs. Smith did not think the matter was quite
so certain, neither did one or two others to whom
Mrs. Stebbings unburthened her mind on the
to her all absorbing subject of Mr. Oscar
Lebrun's "transmogrification" as she called it.
But Mrs. Stebbings held to her own belief, and
thought her daughter had been very much neg-
lected, and, indeed injured, by the young man,
who might have made her his own for the
asking, but had been insincere and treacherous
enough to have had a previous courtship, and
"on the sly," too, as she phrased it, which was
not right for a gentleman as was a gentleman.

Of course all the workpeople in Mr. Haughton's employ had heard the news, and a group of them, taking advantage of the dinner-hour, had congregated in the street opposite Mr. Little's door, to catch a glimpse of their fortunate comrade on his egress from the lawyer's sanctum.

Oscar, unaware of the publicity that had been given to his affairs, or that anyone but Mr. Little knew that he was in the town, was surprised to see the crowd that had gathered, and still more surprised at the loud cheer that greeted his appearance in the street. Even greater than his surprise was his annoyance, when one Simpkin, a discredit to the factory, a workman who made it a rule to get drunk every Saturday night and lie in bed all Sunday to sober himself, stood forward from the rest to wish him joy on his good fortune, expressing a hope at the same time that he would remember his old comrades so far as to stand treat to the whole shop, that they might drink his Lordship's good health.

"I'm not a Lord, as yet, and I don't want to be called 'My Lord.' I don't like it," replied Oscar, with some asperity. "As regards the treat, I'm as poor as any one of you at this moment, and can't afford it. But all the same I'll owe it to you, and pay you the next time I come to Swinston, if any good fortune attends me."

"Honour bright?" asked Simpkin.

"Honour bright!" replied Oscar. "Good-bye. I have to catch the train to London."

"Well, you'll shake hands, old fellow, won't you?" said Simpkin, "and not be proud, even if so be as you are a Lord?"

"I hope I am not so proud, or ever will be so proud, as to refuse to shake hands with any honest and sober working man," said Oscar, with a wilful emphasis on the word "sober," which the bystanders understood, though Simpkin did not; and amid a whole volley of hand-shakings, he emancipated himself from his former comrades, and jumping into the omnibus that was making its way to the railway station, was speedily out of their sight.

" I like the English working people very well," he thought to himself, " but should like them very much better if they had not such a constant hankering after beer, and did not cringe and sneak and beg to get it at the expense of other people."

But he soon banished the subject; and as the express rattled rapidly along towards London, his whole mind, and soul, and thought, and hope were concentrated upon Euphemia Haughton and his approaching interview with her father. As regarded Euphemia he was all hope, all ardour, all confidence, all certainty; but as regarded her father, his doubts were many and strong.

He stood towards him in altered relations. He had scarcely ever exchanged words with him, save of common courtesy and on the strict details of his craft and business. He was a man into whose mind he had never

penetrated, and of whose possible feelings towards anyone who had so unexpectedly come
between him and an inheritance he was wholly
uninformed.

"If he be prejudiced against me for what I
was, and perhaps still more prejudiced for what
I am, I will trust Euphemia still," he thought
to himself; "in her is my hope and my salvation!"

It will be seen that Oscar Lebrun was not
mercenary. He was romantic, he was tender,
he was true, and he was independent—independent, not because of the money that might or
might not come to him, but because of his strong
right hand, his indomitable will, of the power to
earn his daily bread, and the still greater power
of living upon half of his earnings.

CHAPTER V.

On Oscar's arrival in Grosvenor Square, full of hope and courage, he found, as he stood on Mr. Haughton's doorstep, that his heart began to fail him. He had his hand on the knocker, and was about to sound the usual rat-a-tat of gentlemen, when he suddenly withdrew it, and, after a moment's hesitation, resolved to take a walk round the square to collect his thoughts.

A man on whom he had once depended for his daily bread was not be looked upon without a certain amount of awe, and if, by no seeking of his own, he had been placed in a position that might possibly wound that man's pride and conflict with his interest, the awe was increased by recollection of the fact. And more than all, that man was the father of a beloved woman, who was dearer to him than rank, fortune, or all that the world could offer.

He desired to stand, not only well, but excellently well, in the opinion of one on whom the brightest part of his fate depended. He had to explain himself to him; he had to ask him, not only to be reconciled to his probably unwelcome kinship, but to demand the hand of his daughter; and when he thought that he might be coldly received or ungraciously repulsed, he was a great deal more than half inclined to procrastinate, to postpone the day of decision, and, in the meanwhile, to feed his heart upon hopes that might be destined to become realities. So he walked around the square, not once or twice only, but three or four times, trying to pluck up resolution, like a timid bather afraid of the cold water.

He approached the knocker once again, and

5 *

once again lost heart, and took yet another turn around the dull, formal, ugly square, in which dwelt the lady of his heart. He plucked up courage at last, felt inclined to run away, but stood firm until the door was opened by a footman in sober coloured livery. He was told that Mr. Haughton was at home, and having sent up his card, was ushered into the waiting-room. The five minutes that passed ere he was summoned upstairs were minutes of disquietude and anxiety, not unmingled with hope and wonder whether he should see Euphemia, or, if he did not see her, whether she would be informed that he was in the house, and what effect the information would have upon her.

At last he was ushered into the drawing-room. He felt his heart beating as he mounted the stairs, and also felt there was a more than usual flush upon his cheeks. On entering he saw a lady seated in an armchair. Making a courteous obeisance, he at once recognised Mrs. Haughton, who rose as he entered and extended her hand.

" Very glad to see you, Mr. Oscar," she said, kindly; " so just be seated and make yourself comfortable till Mr. Haughton comes ben. He is writing in the library, and will see you immediately."

She looked at him attentively all the time she spoke, and mentally considered whether he were handsome or not, whether she liked him or not, whether he were a gentleman or not, whether he were intelligent or not, and whether he would do honour to his new station or not. On all these points her opinion was more or less favourable.

" And so you 're to be the new Lord Ravelstone, Mr. Oscar?" she said; " and you 're one of the Haughton family?"

" Madame, I am so informed," he replied ; " and however much you and Mr. Haughton may be surprised, I can assure you that I am more surprised than he or anybody else can be."

He might have gone on to say more, but at

that moment Mr. Haughton entered. Oscar rose and accepted the hand which his late employer offered him. Mr. Haughton, not being a lawyer, like Mr. Octavius Little, did not think it incumbent on him to affect doubts which he did not feel. He was quite convinced that Oscar was the grandson of his father's brother, Arthur, and, in consequence of the melancholy death of Lord Ravelstone and his young son, the true heir to the family honours.

He scarcely felt so much as the shadow of a disappointment in the matter, and, in fact, he was rather glad than otherwise to be able to retain his seat in the Commons, which he prized so highly, and that he was not, as the Parliamentary slang has it, " to be pitchforked into the House of Peers." So he said, somewhat paternally, after the hand-shaking was over,

" Pray sit down, Mr. Oscar. I am very glad to make more intimate acquaintance with you than previous circumstances permitted. How could I have suspected that you were a kinsman? "

"How indeed?" asked Oscar. "I know that I never suspected it myself, and that I feel much at a loss in my new position. I do not even know whether you recognise me in that position."

"Oh yes; I believe there isn't the slightest doubt about it. Make yourself at home. You have already formed the acquaintance of my wife, who, as you will see, if you have not already seen, bears no grudge against you for having come between her and 'the wind of her nobility.'"

"I'm no that sure," said Mrs. Haughton, "if I were not a wee bit disappointed; but that's blown awa'. If the lad's to be a peer, he canna help it, ye ken. It's no his fault."

Oscar, after this wholly unexpected cordiality, which relieved his mind of a heavy load, very ardently desired to ask after the young ladies, and whether he might not be permitted to see them; but he forbore. Mr. Haughton went on to say,

"Mr. Little is engaged in some formal matters

connected with your identity, which will not take much time. When he has satisfied his legal conscience, I propose that you should come here —say this day week—to be formally presented to the remaining members of the family, to my daughter Euphemia, whom you know already (Oscar felt his cheeks tingle), to her sister Esther, to my son Herbert, whom you met in Paris, to my brother Colonel Haughton, to Lady Ravelstone and her young family, to my sister Lady Wyld, and her husband Sir Lancelot, and last, but not least, to my highly venerated mother. We shall have a family gathering, and you will be able to judge how you like us."

" Mr. Haughton," said Oscar, " your kindness overpowers me, and almost deprives me of words to reply. I thought you were a cold, and a hard man in the factory. Forgive me an error which was solely the result of my ignorance, and the distance that separated us."

" The factory is one thing, and my own house is another. No man is the same in his office,

or in his shop, as he is at home, among his
family and his friends. But you will come
this day week, at seven?"

"It is my duty, and it will be my pleasure,"
said Oscar, rising, as if he thought the renewal
of the invitation were a hint that the visit had
been sufficiently prolonged.

Mr. and Mrs. Haughton rose at the same
time.

"I would ask you to remain yet a while,"
said Mr. Haughton, "but the fact is I am due
at the House, and you must excuse me if I
run away."

Mrs. Haughton had imagined that her daughters would come down, but as her husband gave
no hint on the subject, she gave none; and
Oscar took his departure, well pleased with the
results of his interview, even though he had
not had the coveted joy of beholding the face
of Euphemia. But as he walked rapidly away,
the beloved one, from an upper window, took
the opportunity of stealing a look at his

retreating figure, but could not see that his features were radiant with satisfaction.

Could he but have known! Ah, we never know! And if he had known, it is just possible that he might have been irresistibly impelled to return into the house, and perhaps render himself liable (to himself) of the charge of indiscretion. But he knew nothing, and consoled himself with the reflection that he was to see her in a week, and that during that week he would not be guilty even of an error—much less of a crime —if he unburthened his soul to her in a letter.

"Blessings on letters!" he said. "I wonder whether the stars do not converse with each other, whether they do not send electric messages from sphere to sphere! What is distance? Nothing. A mere idea, of no mathematical value, or tangible or ponderable importance. I am afraid I am intoxicated with joy. The distance between Euphemia and me seemed at one time to be almost as great as that between the earth and the sun. Now it is nothing. The electricity of Fate has brought us close together, and a penny and a few hours will enable us to speak even more confidentially than we could have spoken in her mother's drawing-room."

He thought the "electricity of Fate" was a vile phrase, but nevertheless he liked it. He thought he was the child of Fate, that Fate had brought him into contact with Euphemia, that Fate had made him love her beyond his own life, and even beyond his hopes of heaven, that Fate had pretended to keep them asunder, and that Fate had very unexpectedly changed its mind, and most generously removed all obstacles. "I almost fear," he thought, quoting the greatest of modern philosophers, "to think how glad I am."

He was walking down Brook Street, on his way to King's Cross and the Great Northern Hotel, when he heard close to his ear a voice which whispered, "Maircann!"

Turning round he saw his French friends Anastase Adolphe and Casimir Desmoulins walking beside him.

"Maireann is fortunate," said the former, "to have a son like you. Two millions and a half of francs! This is a goodly sum to put into the common fund for the organisation of labour, and the regeneration of society. We hear that that is the value of the inheritance into which you have floated. We congratulate Maireann. We congratulate you that you have become so able to help her."

"And no doubt so willing!" added Desmoulins.

Oscar was much annoyed at this *rencontre*, and especially at the confident manner in which his old companions spoke. His love for Maireann had cooled a little. He was not quite sure, as the two Parisians seemed to be, that "Maireann" would reap the benefit of the wealth that had so unexpectedly flowed in upon him. Love for one dear woman had modified his ideas about love for the whole human race, and he felt more than half inclined to resent the too-confident assurance with which his communistic friends addressed him.

" Will you not come with us to the Place of
Leicester Square?" said Desmoulins.   The
Associate Brothers of Industry have a meeting
this afternoon—you know the house?—and they
will be glad of your company. We are in London
on purpose to meet you; we only arrived from
Paris this morning.   You are wanted, brother
Oscar, very much wanted.   Come with us."

Oscar found himself, as the conversation proceeded, walking between the two—as if he had
been a debtor in the custody of a brace of
sheriff's officers. escorting him politely into
durance.   It was best, under the circumstances,
to submit, so he went quietly along with them,
resigned to his temporary fate.

He felt that he was living a double life, and
playing two irreconcilable parts—parts that he
could not continue to play, parts that were more
incompatible than oil and water, for these,
though they cannot assimilate, can dwell together in peace, while his two lives and two
parts were in chemical antagonism, and could

not dwell together in the same retort without either amalgamation or explosion. Amalgamation was impossible; for how could an ardent lover—happy in his love, and with rank and fortune to set the loved one in the high place of the world where it would be his delight to behold her—be at the same time a Communist, holding matrimony to be slavery, and private property public robbery. These thoughts passed rapidly through his mind as they walked along the crowded streets towards Leicester Square.

At last they arrived at the door of a small French restaurant in a side street, dingy, shabby, and almost squalid in outward show, but comfortable within, and in which good cookery, better than that customary at the most pretentious of English eating-houses, and good Bordeaux wine at two shillings a bottle, superior to that for which most English hotels would think it no shame to charge twice the money, were to be obtained.

" *Allons dejeuner!* " said Desmoulins, entering the public room on the first floor, " and we can proceed to business afterwards. The citizen brothers have not yet arrived, but they will be here shortly. What say you, citizen Oscar?"

Oscar would willingly have refused the *dejeuner* on the plea of want of time, or of prior engagements, but he saw no means of escape that would not be unpleasant, and thought it as well to attend the meeting of the "circle" to which he was affiliated, and learn once for all what was expected of him under the new and wholly unexpected circumstances in which he was placed. In enrolling himself among the mystic brotherhood of the Commune his sole object had been the elevation of the working classes, by which he meant the vast majority of mankind, an elevation that he thought might be promoted, if not secured by mutual co-operation for the production and equitable distribution of the physical wealth which he thought Nature and Nature's God intended for the enjoyment of the whole human race; but he had no idea of shutting himself out from love and marriage, and the family relationship. He recognised in his own mind, as he questioned himself, that he was not a Communist, as the word was understood by the leading spirits of the Society; that he would not reduce all men to the uniformity of bees in a hive; that if humanity in the aggregate had rights to enjoy and duties to perform, man in the segregate had rights and duties, the right of being himself and of enjoying his own individuality, commingled with the duty of acknowledging in all other men the rights that he claimed in and for his own person.

It is true that when in receipt of his well-earned weekly wages he had thought that by what he considered a necessary and proper re-arrangement of the relationship between capital and labour, and by the education of the humblest, all other labourers might be raised to the same high level as that on which he himself stood; and without wholly relinquishing that idea, as a theory that some day or other might be made to crystallise into a fact, he was not altogether prepared, now that Fate or Fortune had placed him on a still higher platform, to descend again to the lower level from which he had mounted, the more especially if the descent, so acceptable as a philosophical idea, was to be accompanied by the relinquishment of the woman he loved, or by her debasement to a sphere to which she was not accustomed, and the consequent destruction of her happiness and his own. No. He loved his fellows, but he loved Euphemia Haughton more. He would do all he could for the advancement of the class to which he once belonged, but he would not renounce his newly-found wealth, which he did not much prize for its own sake, but for the sake of her, the Princess, the Queen, the Empress of his thoughts, whom he would not drag down into that inferior station where possibly she might perish, and where, at all events, the fine flower of her delicate beauty might be exposed to the cold blasts of poverty and hardship.

III. 6

With all these thoughts in his mind, crossing and re-crossing each other like the patterns in a kaleidoscope, he consented to breakfast with his Parisian friends, with the more readiness because he was told that the venerable and venerated M. Victor Rabagaud, the Patriarch, the Nestor, and the Mentor of the cause had promised to join them, and was momentarily expected.

M. Victor Rabagaud soon made his appearance and shook hands cordially with Oscar. He was a man who had passed more than a quarter of a century in prison for political offences, and who was now about eighty years of age. But neither age not captivity had borne severely upon him. He stood firm and erect, with a ruddy face, a keen, bright eye, of bluish grey, and long, snow-white hair, and massive beard, slightly tinted with golden yellow at the ends. He appeared so hale and strong as to justify the belief that he might become a centenarian.

Oscar, who met him for the first time, looked upon him with the reverence that the disciple

feels towards the apostle, and admired the pre-
cepts that fell from his lips, even though he
found that he could not always agree with them.
During the *dejeuner* the old man talked much and
well, and almost monopolised the conversation,
if conversation that could be called which was,
de facto, a monologue, only interrupted by remarks or questions that were projected into the
ramparts of his discourse for the sole purpose of
provoking the cannonade of his replies.

"There has been too much talk," he said,
"of the Organisation or the Re-organisation of
labour. What is wanted is the re-organisation
of society upon the principles of Jesus, who,
more than eighteen hundred years ago, desired
to establish a new religion, but could not make
his disciples understand its first principles. They
had, it is true, a feeble comprehension of the
Commune, and made an attempt to organise it,
on the principle that all wealth ought to be public,
not private, and that all men, women, and children were entitled to share alike in the gifts of

6 *

Nature, that were meant for all. Jesus distinctly
told the rich young man who wanted to become
his disciple, to dispose of all his wealth among
the poor; but the young man was not equal to
the duty, and could not, therefore, become a
Christian.   In the triumph of the principle of
the Commune lies the triumph of the human
race over such narrow ideas as patriotism, property, priestcraft, and aristocracy.   What right
has anybody to call himself a patriot and pretend
to love one particular country more than all
other countries, merely because he happened to
be born in it?   A man might just as well call
himself a villager because he was born in a
village, and maintain on that account that his
village was the centre and masterpiece of the
universe, and bound to be right, even if all the
rest of the world was against it.   I detest the
idea of patriotism, which is but another name
for vanity and selfishness, and opposed to all the
teachings of Jesus, whom nearly half the world
pretends to believe in and to worship, though

they set all his teachings at defiance. He was
the foe of priestcraft, yet very odious systems of
priestcraft have been built up in his name.
He was opposed to public prayer, yet in all
the churches of Europe and America public
prayers are constantly paraded, in some countries every day, in others every seventh day,
and all in the name of Him who emphatically
denounced prayer, because God and Nature
knew better how to give, than man knew how to
ask, and who only yielded so far to the prejudice,
that made some men like to pray as other men
like to hear music, as to say to His disciples, that
if any one among them found the necessity of
praying, he should shut himself up in his
closet and pray secretly. In the true Christian
Commune there shall neither be prayer nor
priestcraft, nor any priests at all, except that
every man shall be his own Pope, his own
Bishop, his own priest, and his own congrega-
tion, and shall worship God in the only possible
way by which he can be worshipped—that is,

by obedience to all his laws, physical, moral, and intellectual.

" The model of future society, he went on to say, will be founded on that of the Bee-hive. Every good city and town in the world will form itself into a Commune, and govern itself as the bees do in the hive. France, England, Spain, Italy, Germany, Russia, Greece, Turkey, shall no more be known, except as the names of facts that have passed away. Nations will have ceased to exist, kings, emperors, sultans. and all the rest of such pernicious tyrants will disappear along with the nations that they have misgoverned."

Oscar timidly ventured to suggest that these ideas were Utopian and impossible of realisation.

" I detest the words ' Utopian ' and ' Impossible,'" replied Rabagaud, emphatically. " Utopia, and better than Utopia, may be established, and though there may be physical, there is no such thing as moral impossibility. It was once thought to be impossible to send a message round the world in a minute, but the thing is done daily. To think it impossible that men can dwell together in peace and harmony, and that every man shall love all other men, and work for the good of all other men as well as for his own, is to consider a man as if he were a wolf!—I beg pardon of the wolves; they love each other, and know nothing of the selfish doctrines of Political Economy, which form the Bible of the rich, and are the oppression of the poor."

"I cannot quite follow you," interposed Oscar; "but I listen that I may learn."

"The roots of Political Economy are the unholy doctrines of private property, especially the proprietorship of land and the interest of money. The proprietorship of land is the root of all evil, the first great robbery committed by kings, priests, and soldiers, to the detriment and enslavement of the people. If the kings, priests, and soldiers who have infested the world for thousands of years had had the power to institute property in, and collect rent for, the sunshine and

the fresh air, they would have accomplished their
purpose !"

"*Très bien, très bien !*" said Desmoulins.

"*Superbement bien !*" said his friend.

Oscar was silent, but not convinced, and found,
as he listened to the eloquence of the venerable
enthusiast who sat before him, that a new light
had entered into his mind as to the ulterior
projects of the mysterious society into which he
had been unluckily enrolled as a member.

He had wished to organise labour for the
benefit of the labourers; but he had no thought
of endeavouring to re-organise society on such
broad and revolutionary bases as these, and his
practical intellect revolted against such theories
as M. Rabagaud had propounded, theories that
depended, he thought, for their whole support
on the eradication of the ineradicable—that is,
the selfishness inherent in the human mind.
He saw that, though a reformer, he was not a
Communist, and began to reflect whether it was
not time that he should dissociate himself from

an organisation with whose objects he was so partially and imperfectly in accord.

There passed a shadow over his face, which his two Parisian friends observed with displeasure, but without much surprise, for they had for some time suspected that his heart was not really in the cause, and that he would have to be watched attentively and managed skilfully if he was to be retained in the membership.

M. Rabagaud continued to expound a few more of the ideas on which the Commune was to be established, to which Oscar listened with attention.

"When we have secured free land for a free people, land as free to all as the air, the sunshine, or the sea, we must break down the mischievous barriers of nationality and language that keep mankind apart, and establish one language, one system of weights and measures, a cheap uniform postage to every country in the world, and cheap telegraphic messages under all the oceans."

"The one language," remarked Oscar, "will take thousands of years to establish, if it can be established at all.   But a universal and uniform system of postage, of weights and measures, and of telegraphy, though difficult, is not impossible; and it would be one of the greatest triumphs that Civilisation ever won over the ignorance and apathy of mankind, if the estranged or indifferent nations could be made to unite for such noble purposes."

"You do not think the idea Utopian, as you call it," inquired Rabagaud, blandly.

"No," replied Oscar, "for the unconquerable selfishness of mankind would see the advantage of it, and would work for its fulfilment."

"Selfishness," added Rabagaud, "is the demon in human nature that it is our business to exorcise and destroy."

"Ah," said Oscar, sighing, "is not evil as indestructible as good?   And how could we know that goodness existed, unless we could measure and contrast it with evil?"

"No doubt," said Rabagaud; "but we must maximise good and minimise evil, and if we cannot reach the hundredth degree of perfection, we can reach the ninety-ninth."

"I wish I could think so," replied Oscar, rising to take his leave, and excusing himself from the duty of taking part in the secret meeting that was to follow the *dejeuner*, on the plea of an engagement from which it was impossible to be released.

M. Rabagaud conceived a somewhat favourable impression of the character of Oscar, but Anastase Adolphe and Casimir Desmoulins made up their minds that he was a traitor.

CHAPTER VI.

THE reverses of the Emperor Napoleon in his war against Prussia were becoming every day more serious, and Oscar Lebrun resolved to spend in Paris the few days prior to his formal introduction to his newly-found relatives. He had old associations to renew, to interrupt, or to break off in France. He had either to reconcile himself to the International Labour League, or if it were the Commune, as described by M. Victor Rabagaud, to dissociate himself from the confraternity at once and for ever.

The new relation in which he stood towards Euphemia Haughton had revolutionised—not alone his fortunes, but his whole intellectual and moral nature. He seemed to feel himself taller, wiser, better, nobler than he had ever been, when he thought of the rapidly approaching day when he was to meet her, not furtively, as in the by-gone times at Swinston, but openly, in the face of all the world, as equal to equal. He had mounted to her height. She had not descended to his; and in the light of his love the low, material earth gleamed in the amber and purple hues of Paradise.

Leaving him to the dreams that filled his mind by day as well as night—and which coloured every moment of his life that was not occupied by the approaching establishment of the Republic in France, and the serious affair of his connection with the Maireann, and the position in which he stood with regard to that powerful body, to which, in the rashness of youth, inexperience, and a hopeful but extravagant philanthropy, he had affiliated himself, we must turn to the little incident that troubled the repose of Miss Esther Haughton, and compelled her to become a stranger to Lord O'Monaghan. Her life had flowed pleasantly hitherto, and would have continued to flow in the same unruffled and sunlit channels that open themselves to the career of youth and beauty, when these are blessed with a fair share of the world's wealth, had it not been for an unwelcome revelation that had been forced upon her. Lady Augusta Pippins, who was reported to know everybody and everything, had announced to her, as a matter that deeply concerned her, that Lord O'Monaghan was positively engaged to be married to an elderly, or, more properly speaking, a very old widow, of no personal attractions, with a fortune of a quarter of a million.

"I have heard of this for some time, my dear," she said, "but I would not tell you anything about it until I was positively sure. I hope you never cared much about him?"

The young lady's eyes flashed with even more than the usual splendour with which scorn and indignation can irradiate the face of a beautiful woman.

"I hate him and detest him, the false wretch!"

"He is not worth hating, my dear," said Lady Augusta; "and I really think you are well quit of him, and hope that you will treat the matter with the contempt it deserves. But here comes your mother, and I must tell her all about it."

Mrs. Haughton received the revelation very calmly.

"My poor bairn," she said, turning to Esther, "I hope you did nae care ower muckle for this fellow. I cared naething about him mysel', and thought he was just looking after the siller he thought your father wad gie ye."

"Exactly so," said Lady Augusta. "He was hunting for ten or twenty thousand pounds, and a lovely young woman along with them. He found two hundred and fifty thousand pounds, and an ugly old woman along with them! so he preferred the two hundred and fifty thousand with all its drawbacks. And I think the lovely young woman has had a fortunate escape."

" Well," replied Esther, " I may have had a lucky escape, but I have been cruelly sold, all the same." And she felt the hot tears trickling down her cheeks as she spoke, not for regret at losing Lord O'Monaghan—for she really hated him at the moment—but of bitter anger at having been fooled and jilted. To jilt was one thing, but to be jilted was something very different.

" Oh, if we could but punish him!"

" As how?" asked Lady Augusta; " by bringing an action for breach of promise?"

" Oh no, no!" said Mrs. Haughton, " that would be greater punishment for Ettie and us than it wad be for him. Oh no, no! never, never!"

Mrs. Haughton had never before been seen so excited; but she calmed down quickly.

" No," she added, " such publicity hurts the women folk more than the men folk. And then ye ken, Lady Augusta, ye canna touch pitch without being defiled, and a gentleman canna fight a chimney-sweep, nor should a leddy, even in a court of law, fight a man who has deceived her. At least, such is my opinion."

"You're quite right, Mrs Haughton," replied Lady Augusta. " All you have to do is to 'cut ' Lord O'Monaghan very severely, though I don't think he 'll give you the chance, but will keep carefully out of your way. A quarter of a million is a sore temptation to an embarrassed man, even though it lies in the lap of a disagreeable old woman."

Mr. Haughton, when the fact communicated by Lady Augusta had been fully confirmed from other sources, though indignant at Lord O'Monaghan's audacity, as he called it, in pretending to make love to his daughter for the sake of the money he thought would be settled upon her, was on the whole not dissatisfied at being rid of his Lordship, whom he had tolerated rather than liked. He was too much a man of the world to be surprised, but the absence of surprise did not prevent him from feeling a certain amount of repugnance.

"I don't think," he said to his son, who had muttered something about a horsewhip, "that there is any weapon better fitted to punish such a fellow than the contempt of all honourable men. Let us wash this dirty linen at home, and breathe no word about it to anybody. I don't think, when her first indignation has subsided, that Ettie will care much about the matter. It has not been more than a slight flirtation on her part, and her heart, I imagine, is still whole and sound. I lent the fellow a thousand pounds a month ago, the more fool I; but I rather think that ere many weeks are over, his Lordship will wish that he had borrowed the money of somebody else." Mr. Archibald Haughton vented a rather vehement objurgation, to give emphasis to his determination.

When the story was told, Miss Euphemia was pained for her sister. Esther herself took the matter coolly after the first day,

and pronounced Lord O'Monaghan to be an
"awful humbug;" declared, moreover, that
she had always thought him so, which was not
exactly the truth, or even a half-way approxi-
mation to it; and expressed, moreover, her fixed
determination never to get married.

"I should think," said her brother Herbert,
with a spice of his father's humour and dislike
of slang, "that that determination of yours is
'awful humbug.'"

"It isn't," said Esther; "it's real earnest.
I will never allow a man to talk to me again.
But I hope that Papa will put the false wretch
in prison about the thousand pounds!"

"There's no imprisonment for debt now,"
said Herbert, "and perhaps he will pay up.
And I think, if we are well quit of him for a
thousand pounds, that we've all had a lucky
escape from a very bad bargain."

"Oh," said Esther, biting her lip, "I wish
he could be punished."

"I am afraid," replied her brother, "we

7 *

should have to enlarge our prisons, and increase our police force, if the law were to take cognizance of such offences as Lord O'Monaghan's."

"It's a shame! a too dreadful awfully nasty shame!"

"Dinna fash yoursel', Ettie," said her mother; "it's nae use greetin' ower spilled milk, especially if the milk were bad! There's plenty o' time before ye, ere ye are married, my dear, and we're a' well quit o' this man Monaghan; sae just say nae mair about it, nor let on that ye ever kenned him ava."

Miss Esther was annoyed with herself, but she managed to forget Lord O'Monaghan in less than three weeks. He had never written to her, or she would have burned his letters, or sent them back to him, or torn them into shreds and trodden them under her high-heeled boots. Yet she felt a kind of self-esteem that she was able to despise him.

It will be seen from this little narrative that

two out of the four love affairs in which the members of the Haughton family were involved had settled themselves. The divine Arabella, the model of all loveliness, and once the paragon and idol of Herbert's artistic adoration, had gone out of his ken, and married a costermonger! And Esther, as she said, had been "sold" by Lord O'Monaghan, and determined never to be "sold" any more. There only remained the loves of Oscar Lebrun and Euphemia Haughton, and those of Lancelot Wyld and pretty Patty Tidy, to run their course for good or for evil.

CHAPTER VII.

OSCAR had not been two days in Paris when he met, on the Boulevards, his relative Colonel Haughton, and his friend MacTavish. The fortune of war had gone cruelly against the Emperor, and the city was in a state of fierce commotion at the receipt of the news of some unknown but crushing disaster. It was on a Saturday evening that the fact, known to General Count de Palikao and the Empress Eugenie, thirty-six hours before, had begun to percolate from the reticent official bureaux into the greedy streets and cafés, and to be received with horror by all Conservative Frenchmen, and with delight by the ultra-Red-Republicans and Communists.

The last forgot the humiliation of their country in
their satisfaction at the defeat of the iron-handed
Emperor, who had kept down the evil passions
of the Parisian mob by a relentless severity that
had lasted for eighteen years, and given prosperity to the shopkeepers, and disgust to the
proletaires and the *doctrinaires* of Socialism.
The little *kiosques* where the newspapers were
sold were besieged by clamorous crowds, who
struggled with each other for first possession of
the journals, or snatched them from the hands
of the vendors by sheer force, whenever they
could approach near enough.   Some of the more
excited spirits mounted upon chairs at the doors
of the cafés and read the news aloud to the multitude.   But the journals contained nothing
positive or authentic, nothing but wild rumours
of a terrible reverse, mingled with counter
rumours of a magnificent victory.

"Come with me," said Oscar to his two
friends, " I think I can ascertain the truth if you
will accompany me to the office of the ' Gaulois.'

The editor is a friend of mine, and will tell me what he knows."

They accepted the invitation, for the thirst of news was great upon them, as on everybody else.

Oscar, with some difficulty, procured admittance to the editorial sanctum, and came out in a few minutes afterwards with the intelligence of the capitulation of the Emperor and all his army at Sedan; the Emperor was a prisoner in the hands of the victorious Prussians, and there was an end of the Second Empire. This was about eight o' clock in the evening, and the Chamber was to meet at midnight to debate on the perilous situation of the country, and to assume or establish some sort of a Government.

The news rapidly spread, and all the details were eagerly discussed by the roaring and maddened crowds that swarmed into the streets. Few eyes except those of the little children were closed that night in Paris.

The morning of the next day, Sunday the fourth of September, was extremely fine, and nearly the whole population of the restless capital turned into the Boulevards and the principal thoroughfares, eager, excited, semi-frantic. The sun shone brilliantly, the air was clear, and, as the day wore on, the crowd seemed as happy as if some grand and unexpected stroke of good fortune had befallen every individual in it. The Parisians, not usually addicted to copious libations of strong waters, broke loose from the restraints of sobriety, and the *absinthe* and the *petit verre* had left traces in the eyes, in the cheeks, and in the behaviour of thousands who raised their loud shout of *"Vive la Republique!"* or, quite as frequently, *" Vive la Commune!"*

Battalions of the National Guard, and troops of glackguard *gamins* passed rapidly to and fro singing the " Marseillaise " in chorus, and interrupting the magnificent chant occasionally by shouts of " *Vive la Commune!* "

It appeared, though few people knew it, that the Republic had been voted by the legislative body at the midnight sitting, and that the Empress Regent had taken flight with her son, and left the government of France to hazard and the mob.

"If I had been a woman, and in her place," said MacTavish, "I would have gone to the Corps Legislatif, taking my little son by the hand, appealing, as a mother no less than as a sovereign, to the chivalry and loyalty of the assembly. They would not have hurt a hair of her head, but would have respected her courage, and accepted her son as Emperor!"

"Bosh!" said Colonel Haughton. "They would more likely have torn her in pieces, or re-enacted the tragedy of the Princess de Lamballe. She did well to escape from such tigers. The cruelty of crowds is proverbial. You remember the passage in Shakespear's 'Julius Cæsar'?

> You blocks! you stones! you worse than senseless things!
> Oh you hard hearts! you cruel men of Rome!
> Knew you not Pompey?"

"Yes, I remember," rejoined MacTavish, "and it well describes the behaviour of Paris at

this moment.   It was the vain-glorious black-
guardism of the Parisian mob which drove the
unlucky Emperor into war, and now, when the
fortune of war has gone against him, and they
should have stuck to him through thick and thin,
and raised new legions to support him, they turn
upon him in execration. Bah! I am of the old
school. I think the French the most fickle, blood-
thirsty, and ungrateful nation under the sun."

"All nations are ungrateful," said Colonel
Haughton; "the man who expects gratitude
from the people is more likely to be starved or
stoned to death, or to be spat upon, if he is not
hanged or guillotined, than to be rewarded for
the benefits he has conferred upon them.   Look
now, at these dastard fools who are climbing up
ladders with hatchets in their hands! See what
the silly beasts are doing ! "

His companions looked, and saw two or three
men in blouses, carpenters or builders, perhaps,
who, mounted on ladders, hammer and chisel
in hand, were chopping off from shop-fronts or

porticoes the arms of Napoleon or the letter N.,
which had notified for years that the shopkeepers who dwelt behind had been purveyors of
something or other to the imperial household.

"What senseless brutes!" said the Colonel.
" Doubtless, if the Emperor's son had succeeded
him, they would have given their eyes, almost,
if they too could have been privileged to put the
Imperial N. over their doors or windows, and
on the invoices of their swindling commodities."

" The French are Republicans at heart," said
Oscar, "and they have longed for the Republic
for three quarters of a century ; it is only their
national spirit that is displaying itself as soon as
the pressure of Cesarism is removed.   These
follies are but safety valves for the popular
anger, which might vent itself in methods much
more unpleasant if it could not be indulged in
this fashion.   But here!   I see a well-known
character haranguing the crowd!   Let us listen
to what he says."

It was Rabagaud, mounted on a chair, his

long white hair and beard glistening in the sunlight that streamed full upon his head and face, who, supported by Adolphe, Desmoulins, and others whom Oscar knew full well, was addressing the crowd with vehement and impassioned speech and gestures, and loud denunciations of the fallen Emperor.

"But what of the Prussians?" said a voice in the crowd.

"The Prussians! the Pandours! the Huns!" exclaimed Rabagaud, turning fiercely towards the interrupter. "The Prussians! who cares for the Prussians? They only made war upon the Empire, and the Empire is gone. If they continue to war against the Republic, which they will not be so *bête* as to do, the Republic will make an end of them—scatter the legions of Prussia like chaff before the wind. The very name of the Republic will act upon them with the physical force of a dozen armies, and the moral force that a hundred kings and emperors could not withstand."

"Was there ever such bosh?" said Colonel Haughton.

"Such drivel!" said MacTavish.

"It is no doubt extravagant," said Oscar; "but our people have a passionate love for the Republic. and they are excited overmuch by their joy at the unexpected collapse of the detested Empire."

"But what Republic do they love?" inquired Colonel Haughton. "The three-coloured, or the red?"

"The red," answered Oscar, "a Republic of which there shall be no President, no false-hearted and self-seeking General, biding his time to convert it into a kingdom, or establish a new despotism on his own behalf, or for his own benefit."

Rabagaud meanwhile continued his discourse, the crowd of listeners continually augmenting.

"They talk of the victorious Prussians," he said; "but what victories have they gained? They have, if we consider it rightly, won no victory for themselves, but for us, the people of

Paris, for us, the people of France. They have annihilated the Empire, they have made an end of Monsieur and Madame Buonaparte, the Enfant de la Balle, and all the rest of the Buonapartes. They have established the French Republic, they have laid the foundations of the Commune. I for one am not afraid to cry ' *Vivent les Prussiens! nos bons amis les Prussiens !* ' I see the approaching day when we shall return the favour they have done us, when we shall help them to overthrow the man called Hohenzollern, who styles himself their king, and establish the Republic in Prussia "

" Yes, and all over Europe," said an eager listener.

" Yes, and all over Europe," continued Rabagaud. " Incited by the glorious example of France, the peoples of all the nations shall arise in their might, and make an end of the obsolete old mastodons and megatheria called kings and emperors ; even Russia and Turkey, where ignorant and presumptuous despots call

themselves Czar and Sultan, and wield an unholy
power, only responsible to the knife or the bullet
of an assassin, shall become Republics or con-
stellations of Republics, and be, for the first
time in the world's history, governed by the
people for the benefit of the people. Yes, my
fellow citizens, my brothers in humanity, the
time is coming—it is is more than the eleventh
hour—when there shall be no more kings, no
more nations, no more patriotism, no more war,
no more pauperism, no more slavery, no more
priestcraft, no more usurers, no more aristocrats,
no more lawyers, no more *bourreaux*, crowned or
uncrowned, no more guillotines, no more golden
money; but when the fruits of all the earth shall
be as free to all mankind as the flowers are to
the bees, when every man shall love each other
man, and when everyone shall have enough to
eat and drink, and shall be clothed in purple and
fine linen, and dwell in the palaces of industry
which he has helped to build for himself and
for his fellows."

" *Vive la Commune !* " shouted by a thousand throats, was the response to the fervent oratory.

Desmoulins at this moment caught sight of Oscar and his English friends as they stood attentively listening, and stepped suddenly to Oscar's side, saying in a whisper,

" You are expected to-night; you know the hour, and the place."

He added no more, but slowly regained his position by the side of the chair from which Rabagaud had just descended.

Amid a cataract of *vivas* another orator prepared to take Rabagaud's place, and dilate still further on the glories of the Commune; but the two Englishmen had heard enough, and moved as well as they could out of the crowd towards the Place Vendome, and the Rue de la Paix, followed by Oscar, who began to feel that the cool blood of his English forefathers was gradually assuming the mastery over the hotter blood of his French maternity.

" I don't believe in Rabagaud and his theo-

ries," said Oscar. " I believe in Louis Blanc and
the organisation of labour. I have no faith in
Proudhonism ; and until men become as bees, I
have no faith in the Commune."

"I fancy," replied the Colonel, "that the
Communards are more like bees in one respect
than they are aware of, and that if they have their
own way, they will one day or other organise a
massacre of the drones, or those whom they consider to be drones, merely because they don't work
with their hands."

" And how long do you think it will be, as a
soldier, you know," asked MacTavish, "before
the Prussians attack Paris ? "

"I should think they will be ready in a
week, either to take it by a dashing *coup de
main* or by a formal siege."

" By a siege most likely ! " replied MacTavish.
" I shall leave to-morrow for England, if I am
not already too late to escape. I have no idea
of being cooped up here like a rat in a cage. And
this mob is so frantic that there is no knowing

whether these fanatical Communists may not turn their arms against their fellow-countrymen, and slaughter one. another in the name of their new gospel according to St. Labour."

"Good phrase, MacTavish!" said the Colonel.

"A better phrase, with more truth in it than you imagine," added Oscar; "and it is a saint, I can tell you, in which its votaries most thoroughly believe—which is more than can be said for all the other saints in the Calendar."

"Yes; and it is the thoroughness of their belief which makes these people so dangerous," replied MacTavish. "A thorough believer will do anything, and would burn any of us at the stake without compunction if his faith prompted him to do so. All the horrors of the Inquisition and its *auto da fe's* were the work of genuine believers."

When Oscar parted with the two Colonels— both resolved to leave Paris on the morrow—he fled the noisy Boulevards, the excited crowd, all the life, bustle and temporary madness of Paris,

8 *

and took refuge in his solitary chamber to discuss within himself; for he began to doubt—
amid the turmoil of quickly-happening events of
historical magnitude—whether he ought to consider himself an Englishman or a Frenchman, a
lover or a patriot, an aristocrat or an artisan,
and whether it were humanly possible to combine
all the six characters in one person.

Had he not been deeply in love it is probable
that he would have considered himself above all
things a Frenchman, a workman, and a patriot,
and that he would have made up his mind,
instinctively and without deliberation, to be a
Frenchman, and a Frenchman only, and a patriot
brimful of ardent desire to fight the Prussians
and to aid in establishing the Republic, and to
help on the great and as he thought the good
and noble cause of the organisation of labour.
But love ? aye, love! As the old Scotch song
says,

> " Love is like a dizziness,
>   And will not let a puir body,
>   Gang about his business."

And love upset all his theories, all his calculations, all his resolves, all his unresolves, all
his determinations, all his dreams ; and the wild
theories of which Rabagaud was the disseminator
and apostle completed the change in his feelings
which love had begun.

He loved and was beloved again, and had the
prospect of an inheritance which would enable
him to lavish every worldly good ·that money
could provide on the woman who was to share
his heart, his life and his fortunes.   And was he
to renounce all this, or even to imperil it, for the
sake of France that could do without him ?   Or
for the sake of a Commune in which he did not
believe, if Rabagaud was its oracle?

He would not, and could not renounce his
idea that, by the wise organisation of labour,
the condition of every labourer in the world
could be improved, and the wealth of all
mankind doubled, trebled, or quadrupled ; but
he could advocate and aid that great cause quite
as well in England as he could in France, quite

as well if he were married as if he remained
single, and better if he were a rich man than he
could if he were a poor one.   He thought moreover that no good had ever been done in the
world by the agency of secret societies, and that
the new position into which he had so unexpectedly been raised, rendered it imperative upon him
to break up the connection he had formed with the
" Maireann," in the doctrines of which he was but
a neophyte, and with the full secrets and purposes of which he was but imperfectly acquainted,
and most of which, as far as he knew or understood, he disapproved, as either absurd and
impracticable, or wholly mischievous, if Rabagaud correctly propounded them.

Another consideration was the approaching
siege of Paris by the victorious Prussians, who
would certainly not stop short at the dethrone-
ment of the Emperor and the collapse of the
Empire, but would carry on the war against the
Republic, unless the Republic sued for peace,
which was utterly improbable.

He had promised to return to London within a week, to meet Euphemia in her father's house for the first time, and if he remained even a day longer in Paris he might find it difficult or impossible to pierce the Prussian lines, in which case he might be separated from his heart's delight, and from all his new-born hopes and joys for an indefinite period. He deplored, as a semi-Frenchman, the misfortunes of France; but love had made an Englishman of him. So he came to the resolution, long before nightfall, that he would leave Paris along with Colonels Haughton and MacTavish, and that he would not attend the meeting to which he had been so suddenly summoned by Desmoulins.

He carried out his resolution in both particulars, and thought himself happy, before a week had elapsed, that he had been prompt enough to act on his convictions.

CHAPTER VIII.

Two days after his arrival in London, and before the time appointed for the family gathering in Grosvenor Square, Oscar received a letter which annoyed him greatly on its first perusal, and filled him with indignation on the second. It was not signed, but he knew too well from whence it came. It reproached him for his non-attendance at the council, when duly summoned by the officials whose business it was to convene the " brotherhood," and hinted that an explanation was imperative, if he would avoid unpleasant consequences. The document was marked with a cross and a death's head, and an " eye," such as is sometimes seen in vulgar representations of the Deity, and bore the motto " Beware ! " But Oscar *was* " aware," and tore the missive into fragments, which he afterwards burned, with a grim resolution to have done with the " Maireann " at once and for ever, and to take the consequences rather than to submit to such tyranny as this.

All the doubts and quasi-doubts, and indeed all possible doubts, as to his birth and parentage having been removed to the complete satisfaction of every member of the Haughton family and their confidential lawyer, Mr. Little, he ceased to be spoken of by any of them as M. Lebrun. To Euphemia Haughton he was simply Oscar, as in the days of yore, but to everyone else in the circle he became known and spoken of as Lord Ravelstone. But he did not call himself a Lord, and thought it rather odd that he should have become one, though he reconciled himself so far to his new circumstances as to re-assume the name of his grandfather. Oscar was a straightforward man, and hated secrecy and concealment quite as much as Mr. Haughton did (and nobody hated them more), and thought it his duty to the gentleman whose daughter he hoped to marry—a gentleman who in his business employed hundreds of men—to explain to him the relationship in which he stood towards the working classes and the Grand International League of Labour. Of the " Maireann," which had grown out of it, and was an *imperium in imperio* in the midst of it, with objects not communicated to what might be called the lay members of the league, but were only known to the high priests of the hierarchy, he did not consider himself permitted to speak.

Mr. Haughton was glad to learn from a superior working man, with whom for the first time he was able to hold confidential intercourse, some of the veiws and feelings of his class.

" Employers and employed," he said, " that is capitalists who have money, and capitalists, if they may be so called, who have no capital but

health, strength, and skill, don't understand
each other in England, or anywhere else. They
stand like bitter foes arrayed against each other,
whereas they ought to consider themselves firm
friends and allies. The capitalist, who has money
to spend in wages, is the root of the tree, and
the workers, who draw sap and sustenance from
the root, are the leaves and branches. This is
not understood by the working men. They
quarrel with the root; and when they do, the
leaves wither for lack of life, and the branches
are unable to expand. You are an intelligent
man, Lord Ravelstone."

"Oscar Haughton, if you please;—for the
present at all events."

"Well, Oscar Haughton, you have mixed with
working men as equal to equal, and been in
their confidence; whereas I have never been
able to exchange a genuine thought with any
person in my employ. I have paid my men
their wages punctually and honourably; but they
have always seemed to hate me, as if I took to

myself more than an equitable share of the pro-
fits of my business, forgetting that an adequate
reward was due to me for supervision, for interest
of capital, for wear and tear of machinery, for my
time, rather more valuable than theirs, for the
chance of bad debts, for which I, not they, are
responsible, for the fluctuations of the market,
and for the competition of rivals, scrupulous or
unscrupulous. They do not, in reality, understand the commonest rudiments of the science of
labour; for labour is a science. They forget that
if Society, or somebody representing Society, did
not save last year's seed, there would be no crops
this year, and that the seed saved by the wise
few is valuable, and has to be bought by the
many who did not save it, and who want to sow
it for their own benefit."

"But," replied Oscar, "the working men, as
far as I know, do not object to capital in itself,
and would very much like to possess it. They
object to individual and private capitalists.
They think that Society, the Government, the

State, or something representing the whole
people, should be the saver and the capitalist, for
the sake of the whole people."

"But what would become, in that case, of the
indispensable eye of the master? The State
could only superintend by means of paid super-
intendents, who could not look at things with the
penetrating watchfulness of what you call the
private capitalist."

"Right or wrong, their idea is that capital is
a tyrant, unless possessed by the community on
behalf of the community."

"But might not the law of gravitation be as
justly called a tyrant?" asked Mr. Haughton.

"The working men," continued Oscar, "have
another notion which I cannot think to be wholly
without warrant, that capitalists and employers,
in their over-hastiness to grow rich, compete
dishonestly with each other, and grind the
workmen down between them. If there are two
bakers or grocers in a street or village, and only
trade enough to support one of them comfortably,

one or both resort to adulteration of goods, or to
short weight and measure, to enable them to live.
But the great complaint of the working men in
the main staples of manufacture in England,
such as those of wool, cotton, iron, steel, and
coal, by which so many hundreds of thousands
of men gain their daily bread, the employers
compete too greedily one with the other, and
'kill the goose that lays the golden eggs.' English
cotton goods are being driven out of the markets
of the world by their worthlessness, and cutlery
that won't cut, although it bears the mark of
Sheffield, is refused even by the aborigines of
Africa."

"Too true," rejoined Mr. Haughton; "and
the workmen who do honest work have a right
to complain of the masters that turn out dishonest work. But where is the remedy?"

"The workmen think they see the remedy in
the system that is known as the Organisation of
Labour, a system to be worked by the labourers
themselves, for their mutual benefit, without the

intervention of an individual capitalist or employer; and the workmen think, as far as I am acquainted with their minds, that they could compete successfully with the great manufacturers, by providing honest goods at the same price charged by the 'shoddy' men for dishonest goods, and so act not alone as good men of business, but as patriots."

"I am sure I wish they could and would," replied Mr. Haughton. "Nobody would rejoice at the result more than I should. But have the working classes patience, courage, sobriety, and self-denial enough to establish such agencies out of their *savings?* Without an accumulated fund of savings they could not carry on a large factory or manufactory for a month."

"That is the real difficulty," said Oscar, "at least in England. The working man's eternal— I had almost said infernal—love of beer stands in the way. Not that I dislike beer; on the contrary, I like it, if it be pure and unadulterated, and taken in moderation. If one hundred thousand workmen, in order to raise sufficient capital to establish a business, would each forego a pint of beer for one day in the week, and carry out their practical abstinence, not a very severe sacrifice, for only six months, they would raise a capital of—let me see—I have made the calculation—of no less than thirteen thousand three hundred and thirty-three pounds and some odd shillings, or nearly twenty-seven thousand pounds per annum. Of course if they would refrain from beer for two days in the week instead of one, the annual sum would be fifty-four thousand pounds. But it is idle talking to them. They won't give up any portion of their beer, they won't combine, and they won't deny themselves the smallest and most unnecessary luxury, for the sake of any cause, however noble. That is the worst of the English. The French and the Germans have more self-control, and sounder notions of the right way to pursue for the elevation of the labouring classes. That is my experience, Mr. Haughton, and, as regards England, my despair."

" Well," said Mr. Haughton, " I am instructed by your remarks, and may introduce some of them into the speech which I intend to make in the House of Commons, while you, as a Peer, a very unique Peer, who has earned his own bread by the sweat of his brow, can instruct the House of Lords at the same time."

" Not so very unique," replied Oscar. " You had the eldest son of a Peer in your employ a short time ago, and nobody knew anything about it but myself—a lad of nineteen, a scape-grace, an independent fellow all the same, with a high spirit, and heir to one of the most ancient families in England. He called himself John Smith, but I knew all about him, and kept his secret. He is reconciled to his father now; and whether he be a Grosvenor, or a Percy, or a Cavendish, a Howard, a Neville, or a Vere de Vere, I am not going to say, he was the equal of any of them."

" Glad to hear of it," said Mr. Haughton. " Glad to hear of such ' pluck ' among the upper classes, and I augur well of the young man's future career."

Mr. Haughton parted from his newly-found relative with feelings of much esteem, and thought that his daughter, who might in her rashness have shipwrecked her whole fortunes, had been happy indeed in having formed an attachment to one who to personal graces added those of the mind, and who promised to be an honour to the family.

Of Oscar's interview next day with Euphemia Haughton in her father's house, as her acknowledged lover, of what use is it to speak? The raptures of lovers—very rapturous indeed, if they be young, hopeful, innocent, and unfretted and uncontaminated by the world and the world's ways—are apt to be uninteresting in the repetition, or to be designated by the heartless and the worn-out as " spooney." The tenderest love-passages in letters that have unfortunately to be read in Courts of Justice, always excite the most laughter. Prosaic and vulgar barristers turn them into ridicule for the amusement of equally prosaic or vulgar juries, and the solemn judge relaxes into a smile whenever the cooings of human doves are recorded. The age in which we live does not approve of the word "love" in every-day conversation, and young ladies and gentlemen have all but ceased to speak or sing of it, as if they had agreed to relegate the public utterances of everything relating to the tender passion to novels, the operatic stage, or negro minstrelsy, in all of which, except in the novels, it partakes more or less of the comic, the unreal, and the silly.

Oscar Lebrun was not ashamed of being in love; he gloried in it, and he loved with all his heart. He was an earnest and not a fashionable young man, and Euphemia Haughton was a genuine and not a fashionable young woman, if the word "fashionable" be employed, in the sense of having lost all appreciation of the natural either in speech or in feeling. To both of them their mutual love was the highest joy the world could

9 *

offer, and so full and complete as to inspire them with a secret and unexpressed presentiment and dread that so much happiness was too heavenly for the earth. They knew, or at least they had every right to imagine, that their love was true, and that its course was running so smoothly as to suggest either that Shakespear's romantic assertion was untrue, or that the very truth of their passion was nothing but a forerunner and an augury of misfortune. But they said none of these things. They did not even think of them when they were together, for the divine light of present happiness was on them and around them. Let us leave them to their joy; let us not repeat to profane ears what they said to each other, if they said much. Perhaps they said very little; for the greatest happiness is not garrulous, and often finds in a look or a touch greater delight than mere language can convey.

The day of the dinner at Mr. Haughton's, in Grosvenor Square, was a day that Colonel

Haughton looked forward to as the crowning triumph of gastronomy, and of the temperate conviviality that should always surround a symposium as the atmosphere envelops the earth.   The great *chef* whom he had recommended to his brother was too great to tolerate hints or suggestions, but he made an exception in favour of the Colonel, who was his patron and protector, the man who believed in him, and who advanced his interests whenever he could. Great man as the "Baron" thought himself, he condescended to take counsel with the Colonel—or rather he allowed the Colonel to take counsel with him, in a rather humble and deferential way—as to the composition and order of the unparalleled *menu* which was to celebrate the introduction to his family of the heir of Ravelstone. I have a transcript of that identical *menu*, which I am selfish enough not to communicate to a careless, an ignorant, or an ungrateful public; but it is and will be at the service of any future *chef* (Baron or no Baron, Count or of no account) who will

humbly sue for a transcript of the precious
document.

The Colonel was somewhat disappointed as to
the results when they appeared on the table ;
but on the whole he was pleased enough, and his
disappointment, such as it was, whether real or
affected, was natural to one who was nothing if
not critical. What is the good of having, or
fancying to have, a superior knowledge of history,
philosophy, the drama, art, poetry, or cooking,
unless you can find fault with the achievements
of other people, always, of course, your inferiors,
who have presumptuously atttempted to excel in
any of those departments of genius?

Oscar, as was but natural on such an occasion,
ran a gauntlet of criticism, personal and im-
personal, of which he was quite unaware. The
general opinion was favourable towards him.
Sir Lancelot Wyld saw nothing horsey about
him, which was a recommendation. The Colonel
thought he was a living proof of the superiority
of "blue" blood over any other kind of blood

—though it was as red as a costermonger's. Mrs. Haughton the elder admired his modesty. Mrs. Haughton the younger was pleased to note the glow of health on his cheeks, and to learn that he disliked smoking. Lady Wyld thought he was passably good-looking, but not to be compared to her boy. Lady Ravelstone looked at him with curiosity, but no other feeling. Miss Esther thought him somewhat old fogeyish and slow. Miss Euphemia thought him a divinity. Mr. Herbert Haughton considered him a good fellow and not stuck up; and Mr. Haughton himself thought he would turn out to be an excellent man of business.

Oscar, on his part, was greatly attracted by the elder Mrs. Haughton, and still more by Euphemia's mother.

One of his characteristics—unfortunately not so common as it ought to be among the male and female youth of the present era, who call their father the " Governor " and their mother the " old woman "—was his genuine respect for old age.

Wicked old age is detestable; but virtuous old age, that bears upon its countenance the placid benignity that cannot be counterfeited, but can only be acquired by life-long cultivation of the best qualities of the intellect and the heart, exacts homage, and receives it willingly from all but the vulgar and the evil-minded.

But ere the evening had closed, Oscar was of the opinion that he had always entertained since he first saw her—that Euphemia Haughton was the loveliest woman that had ever walked the earth, and that next to Euphemia was her mother.

"Fools and human parrots," he thought, "that speak without thinking, and that follow in the well-worn track of the stupid and imitative multitude, are always levelling their pointless jokes against the mothers of their wives. I am grateful to the mother of her who is to be my wife for having brought into the world such a paragon of loveliness and goodness; and if a human donkey presumes in my presence to speak disrespectfully of his own wife's mother, or of the mother of any other person's wife, I will, if he be an acquaintance of mine, drop him out of my list, and if he be not an acquaintance, shall refuse to make him one."

In the evening, after the dinner, Mrs. Haughton, acting upon the advice of her old friend Lady Augusta Pippins, had a reception, the names of the persons attending which appeared on the following morning in the "Morning Post," and filled fully half a column of that journal.

Lady Augusta found occasion during the evening to have a little quiet talk with Mrs. Haughton, as they sat for a few minutes in the conservatory, on the subject of O'Monaghan.

"I dare say," she remarked, "that Mr. Haughton was both surprised and disgusted with his mercenary behaviour and the heartless way in which he had trifled with poor Esther."

"No," replied Mrs. Haughton; "he was indignant, but not surprised."

"Neither was I," said Lady Augusta; "indeed, at my time of life, my dear, I am not surprised at anything, except at some deed of great and unexpected heroism and virtue, which very seldom occurs. And how does your daughter continue to take it? Is she disappointed?"

"Not the wee-est wee bit," replied Mrs. Haughton. "She was angry that he should have dared to propose to her; but the anger wore awa', and left naething behind it but a cauld contempt; and it's weel it should be so."

Nothing further was said, and the two ladies rose and mingled with the rest of the company. Lady Augusta's sharp eye caught sight of Ettie, seated on a sofa, with a florid and handsome young man beside her, with luxuriant black hair and whiskers, faultlessly regular white teeth, and with delicate hands such as any damsel might have been proud of. He was evidently a clergyman, by his attire, and was engaged in earnest discourse with his fair companion.

"Who's the young man?" inquired Lady

Augusta, in a whisper to Mrs. Haughton, putting her gold eye-glass to her eye as she spoke.

"Only the Reverend Hope Smithers, the curate of Swinston. Ettie refused him once; but I'm thinking he's plucked up courage to ask again since he heard that things hae gane wrang about O'Monaghan."

"High or broad—rich or poor?" inquired Lady Augusta, again putting her gold eye-glass to her eye to have a better look at the young gentleman.

"Amaist as high as St. Peter's at Rome amaist as poor as Job," replied Mrs. Haughton, in her very broadest Scotch.

The company that evening was both numerous and miscellaneous. Lady Augusta Pippins tried to bring a duke under her wing, but was not able to manage it. She succeeded, however, with two earls, a viscount, a baronet, and four younger men entitled to be called "the Honourable."

The representatives of art, literature, science, and of high commerce mustered strong. There was Mr. Wordy, the great novelist; and Miss Babble, also a novelist, who wrote a novel in three volumes every month; Mr. Misty, a celebrated but not a popular poet; Mr. Tantipori, without a wife, and said to be worth a million of money; Herr von Blitzen, the great electrician; Mr. Verjuice, the rising young man from Oxford, who wrote all the savagest articles in the "Scarifier," and who, by virtue—or vice—of his ill-nature, was held to be an authority on every subject whatsoever, and to have the making or the unmaking of every literary or artistic aspirant in his hands; Miss Doctor Obstetrica Jones, from New York, with blue spectacles and a red nose, who asserted in her public lectures on Medicine and Surgery—to which no men were admitted—that man midwifery was a scandal to the age and the female sex; and Dr. Anastasius Timperley, who said he could float in the atmosphere with

as much facility as a herring in the Atlantic, and
could summon at will any departed spirit that
had ever inhabited the earth, to answer any
questions that he, or anyone who employed him,
chose to put to him. There were also a great
Roman Catholic Monsignore, and the Rev.
Joshua Prodgers, who made such charming
discourses to the costermongers, and had actually
persuaded five or six of them to refrain from
kicking their wives and ill-treating their donkeys.
There were at least a dozen Members of Parliament and their wives and daughters; and two or
three foreign gentlemen, who either sang or
played ; and a brace of the Club acquaintances
of the Colonel, of whom one was Colonel Mac-
Tavish and the other the old and irascible
Admiral, his brother, to whose memory of his
own past history the family of the Haughtons
were indebted for the faint but certain clue that
led to the discovery of the lost Lieutenant, the
grandfather of the new Lord Ravelstone.

Mr. Haughton, though he had enjoyed the

dinner well enough, was woefully weary of the
" reception," and would have much preferred a
quiet rubber, or even a snooze upon the sofa;
but then he thought that his position as a
Member of Parliament entailed certain social
duties upon him, and he resigned himself to the
tyranny of Colonel Haughton, aided in this
matter by Lady Augusta and his wife. He was
glad, however, when the last guest had departed,
and still gladder to think that there would be
no repetition of the performance for at least a
month.

That night Miss Ettie Haughton confessed to
herself in the solitude of her chamber that the
Rev. Hope Smithers improved upon acquaintance,
that he was younger and better-looking than
Lord O'Monaghan, and that he was by no means
such a fool as her father thought him. That
night her sister Euphemia was prouder and
happier than she had ever felt in her life.

CHAPTER IX.

In the Haughton family in London things went on pleasantly—as calmly, perhaps, as the torrent's smoothness ere it dash below. Mr. Haughton was constant in his attendance in his beloved Parliament, and though he had never caught, or attempted to catch, the Speaker's eye, he was looking out for an opportunity to make a great speech on some great question, which opportunity, however, did not arrive in the course of that Session, but was confidently hoped for in the next.

Oscar and Euphemia Haughton were betrothed, and their marriage was appointed to be solemnised within a period of six months, which Oscar would gladly have shortened to six weeks or six days if he could have obtained consent.

Though Mr. Haughton was of the opinion expressed in the old proverb, "Happy is the wooing that is not long a-doing," he thought that in this case there were family reasons for delay. The young people would do well, in his opinion, to know each other better in courtship, and to enjoy that happy oasis in the world's wilderness before taking the irrevocable step.

Lord O'Monaghan darkened Mr. Haughton's doors no more, and the Rev. Hope Smithers, taking his opportunity from that circumstance, laid violent siege to the not very well defended citadel of Miss Ettie's heart, with such apparent success on one day, and with such apparent want of success on another, as to leave his not very brilliant mind in some degree of doubt whether or not the fair lady were amusing herself with him and extracting pastime from his company.

But about this time the festival of St. Grouse

had come round again, and the Parliamentary
Session came perforce to a close. The legis-
lators swarmed to the moors, or to the Continent,
and London was declared to be quite empty,
though out of its four millions of people perhaps
no more than thirty or forty thousand in all had
deserted its busy thoroughfares.

But those thirty or forty thousand called
themselves " Society," the world, the fashion,
the everybody, the everything, the cream of the
cream, and, as it were, the very quintessence of
the salt of the earth.

Mr. Haughton betook himself and his family
to the mill; for had they not had their coveted
holiday in the Metropolis? and was it not
wholesome for mind and body to be at home
sometimes?

Oscar Lebrun—for he had not yet assumed
the title that belonged to him—resolved to visit
his mother at Margaux, and take leave of his
French relatives ere finally settling down as an
Englishman; and as he could not travel through

Paris—invested and besieged by the victorious Prussians, and "stewing in its own gravy," as the grimly - facetious Bismarck irreverently expressed it—he resolved to travel by steamer direct to Bordeaux, and, until his return from this act of filial duty, to maintain a constant correspondence with Euphemia.

How he wished that he could have taken her with him as his wife, to present her to his mother, and dazzle the good woman's eyes by her new daughter's loveliness! But this could not be until six months had elapsed, and he would not be absent more than as many weeks. Meanwhile he would feed his heart on sweet hopes and glowing wishes, and talk to his beloved with his pen, and say, perhaps, things more fervent and more eloquent than he could have uttered with his lips.

Mr. Herbert Haughton accepted a berth in the yacht of Mr. Smith Smeaton, the younger partner in an engineering firm, who proposed a six weeks' cruise among the islands of the Hebrides, and perhaps as far as Norway.

Colonel Haughton lingered in town, almost the last man in his Club, reigning, as it were, the autocrat of that establishment, ruling the cook, the butler, and the waiters with a rod of iron, and monopolising their services, while ignorant of the fact that they all wished him at Jericho, or a hotter place, for presuming to remain in town, when everybody who aspired to be anybody had gone out of it.

Lady Wyld, weary of the village in which her husband did his clerical duty, wanting a change from the usual round of visits to poor old paupers, from the distribution of coals, blankets, and gruel, and from the work which usually falls to the lot of Rectors' and Vicars' wives, had made up her mind that she would not go to any English watering-place; that she would not go to the Highlands, either of Wales or Scotland; that she would not go to Switzerland or the Tyrol (she could not go to the Rhine or France on account of the Franco-Prussian war); that she would not go to Rome, or Naples, or Algiers, or Egypt, all

10 *

of which places were suggested by Sir Lancelot, but that she would go to the United States of America, and nowhere else.

This was a proposition that both startled and annoyed Sir Lancelot, and was debated between the pair for two or three weeks, with more or less of obstinacy on his side and acrimony on hers. " Ce que femme veut, Dieu veut," says the proverb; but Sir Lancelot, if the truth must be told, was of opinion that " le Diable " was the real person meant in this hackneyed saying, and that the woman's will, being, as it were, the Devil's, ought to be resisted, the more especially if the man's will ran in a contrary direction.

But in spite of the ponderous resistance of Sir Lancelot, Lady Wyld calculated that if she only persevered she would conquer at last. She ardently desired to see her son. She was miserable without him, and had made up her mind that he had been harshly treated.

She thought, moreover, that he might be ill in a strange land, with nobody to nurse him or take care of him.   And why couldn't she go to America ?   Her mother was an American, and it was to some extent the land of her ancestors. And why shouldn't Sir Lancelot go?

If he didn't care to see his own son, which was very unnatural on his part—but then, she thought, he always was unnatural when poor Lancelot was concerned—she was certain that a sea voyage would do both him and her good; not a little miserable trip from Dover to Calais, but a good ten or twelve days of it from Liverpool to New York; and, moreover, every English gentleman of any position at all ought to round up his experiences of English public and political life by a similar experience of America.   She heard everybody say so.

No one, she was informed, was fit to be a Member of Parliament, and to pass an opinion on the democratic tendencies of the age in England, who had not studied those democratic tendencies in action across the Atlantic, among men of the same race and speaking the same language; and if a Member of Parliament, why not a Baronet, a country gentleman, and a clergyman?

Sir Lancelot, to whom all these questions, and many others, were put in various forms every day—almost every hour—failed to see the force of the arguments. He said he was too poor, said he could not be spared from his parish, said he was a wretchedly-bad sailor, said he hated America, said it was a country in which there was nothing to be seen or learned, said the climate was detestable, and gave a hundred other reasons which he thought equally cogent, why a visit to the United States was out of the question.

Lady Wyld ventured to urge that if the climate were so very detestable, it was neither a paternal nor a kind proceeding on his part to banish his poor unoffending son to such a place. Sir Lancelot took objection to the words " poor," " unoffending," and " banish," but felt all the while that he was fighting a losing battle. He

knew that the plea of his own poverty for such
a journey was unavailing, for his wife had money,
and would pay. He knew also that he could be
as well spared from the parish for a voyage to
America as he could be for a tour on the Continent of Europe, in which he had often before
indulged; that an orthodox and gentlemanly
curate, acceptable to the ladies and the congre-
gation generally, could be secured for a very
small sum to officiate in his absence; and that
there were really no arguments he could use in
opposition to those of his wife, except one, that
he did not wish to go, which on reflection he
admitted was no argument at all. It is true he
had another idea, which he kept in the background
of his own inner consciousness, and which he had
not courage enough to divulge to Lady Wyld,
which was that a visit to his scapegrace of a son
would impress that young gentleman with a much
too high opinion of his own importance, and un-
settle him for his life in America, before he had
had half enough of time to subside into habits

of industry and self-reliance, or to cast off the slough of his old associations of the betting ring.

The warfare between the married pair lasted with more or less of acerbity from day to day; sometimes it was an open quarrel, sometimes a mere nagging match, sometimes a quasi-friendly but really hostile argument, sometimes on the lady's side an appeal *ad misericordiam*, in which the Baronet was slightly shaken from his stern purpose. But as the weeks wore on, he was aware that he was gradually getting the worst of the battle, and began to debate in his own mind whether it would not be better either to surrender at once, or consent to a compromise. He soon found, however, that any compromise was impossible, that Lady Wyld meant America, and would in all probability go to America alone, if he refused to accompany her ; for he knew very well from experience that if she were weak in many things, she was strong in everything that regarded her son.

He thought he was lord and master, absolute and above parley, in his own household; but

he wasn't. This delusion the worthy man shared
with possibly ninety if not ninety-nine per cent.
of his parishioners, and if his parish had included
the whole of the civilised word, the per-centage
might not have been very much below that
average. But nevertheless he clung to it in a
hazy, half-hesitating way, convinced by the little
unimportant things in which he conquered—but
taking no account of the great things in which
he was too often routed, " horse, foot, and artillery "—that he was the real lord and master.

" Lancelot," said the lady to him one morning
at breakfast. And as she usually called him *Sir*
Lancelot, he thought that her tenderness in
dropping his title and calling him only by his
Chistian name, portended an attack upon him on
a weak point; and he was right. " Lancelot,"
she said in a plaintive tone, " you loved me once,
and if you love me still, you will take me to
America, to prevent my falling ill, and dying."

Sir Lancelot was not alarmed; he did not
think his wife would fall ill, or if she did, that

she would die; but he began to think that he
might make up his mind to undertake the
journey with a good grace. After all, the United
States was an interesting country, in which
there was much to be learned, and he might
enlarge his knowledge and improve his mind by
a short visit to New York, Washington, Rich-
mond, and New Orleans, before the winter.

Lady Wyld was a good wife, a little infirmity
of temper excepted, and if she had set her heart
earnestly upon a thing which was not, after all
was said, either unnatural or unreasonable, it
would do him no harm to gratify her. Besides,
she might take it into her head to go to America
alone, and the best way to prevent such a catastrophe was to accompany her. Finally he consented to undertake the journey, and to commence his preparations on the morrow.

Lady Wyld was radiant with satisfaction, and
rising from her seat, put her arms round her
husband's neck, and kissed him. It was not often
that she relaxed her dignity so far as this, and

Sir Lancelot, not over-pleased at what he considered to be no more than the seal and graceful recognition of his defeat, and not altogether a proof of any abiding or even reviving tenderness towards him, received the tribute as if it were his due, and consoled himself with the reflection that he had at least purchased peace for a while by his tardy concession.

But the preparations for the journey had not advanced very far when Sir Lancelot found occasion to remember that other French proverb which says, "L'homme propose, mais Dieu dispose," and to think that after all he might not visit the United States. The disturbing element in his calculations was the receipt by Lady Wyld of a letter from her son, dated New York, in which he announced his intention of taking passage for England by the next steamer. This startling announcement filled the Baronet with indignation, and the clergyman with grief, but at the same time filled the mind of Lady Wyld with unmitigated and unexpected joy. Lancelot informed his mother, and through her his father, that he had no intention of quitting America altogether, that he liked the country "awfully," that the life of a planter and horse-breeder in Virginia suited him "immensely," and that he only returned to England to make arrangements with her and his father for a permanent residence in a country where, with a little assistance, he thought he could make his fortune. There was, he added, another little matter which it was his desire to explain in person.

Sir Lancelot was in a perverse humour.

"I shall go to America all the same," he said. "I want to see the country, and to study it; and I don't see why my intentions should be frustrated by the unaccountable whims and caprices of this horsey boy."

"Well, Sir Lancelot," said his lady, meekly, "you can go if you please. I don't want to interfere with your movements, and I really think the voyage would do you good. But of course you will stay to receive Lancie? Not that it matters! But it would look better if you did; and the arrangements of which he writes may be more important than we think."

"I know him better than you do, Lady Wyld," said her husband; "and it is my impression, and a strong one, that he is coming back for no other purpose than to sneak around Patty Tidy."

"Sneak!" said Lady Wyld. "As if *my* son could sneak! It is not in his nature, Sir Lancelot, and I don't believe he cares for Miss Tidy in the slightest degree."

"And it is my belief that he does, in a very great degree, and that he is an infatuated fool and ass!"

Lady Wyld bit her under-lip.

"You know, Sir Lancelot, what an ass's father must be."

Sir Lancelot remembered this very old joke, and as its application to himself was not complimentary, and was not intended to be, he thought it discreet to take no notice of it. He went on to say as if he had not been interrupted,

"You wilfully shut your eyes, Lady Wyld.
I keep mine open, and I see that the boy is
crazy about this girl, and that if he be not
taken vigorously in hand he will do something
desperate."

"Desperate! what do you mean?"

"I mean that he will marry her, and that he
is coming from America for that purpose. Of
course he will marry somebody sometime, though
there is no positive necessity; but that he should
marry so far beneath him is unfortunate. You
will at least admit as much as that, Lady Wyld?"

Lady Wyld was, perhaps, of the same opinion;
but she was angry with her husband for inter-
posing his objections between her and the full
joy she anticipated from the sight of her son, and
argued against her own convictions in order to
annoy Sir Lancelot.

"I don't know," she said, "that Lancie cares
particularly for the girl. No doubt he admires
her—for I must say she is good-looking, and
fresh, and well-behaved—but between admiring

and marrying there is a wide distance.   But even if he were to marry her, I don't think any such mighty harm would be done."

" But the daughter of a village blacksmith— in our own village too ! "

" Well," said his lady, " I don't particularly object to blacksmiths.   Why should I—or you either ?   You know my brother is only a big blacksmith, after all, and an employer of some hundreds of blacksmiths; and you—you know, married a blacksmith's sister."

" It is not so much that the man is a black- smith," replied Sir Lancelot, testily, and not liking the argument or the illustration.   " All men are equal in the sight of God, and it would ill-become me in my sacred profession to look down upon the man Tidy, merely because he follows the avocation which he understands, and to which he has been brought up; but he dis- believes in the Mosaic account of the Creation."

" Well, as for that," replied Lady Wyld, " I am not certain that I do not disbelieve in it too."

This was too much for Sir Lancelot.

"Madam," he replied, with a severe and solemn tone, "I will pray to the Lord for you, and that He will be graciously pleased to turn your heart to the truth!" And he left the room angrily and banged the door after him.

Lady Wyld took no notice of this outburst of temper, but proceeded to read her son's letter again. This having done, she kissed it, folded it, placed it in her bosom, and went into the garden to attend to her roses and geraniums, and think of Lancelot.

CHAPTER X.

Sir Lancelot Wyld understood his son's character; Lady Wyld's partiality blinded her to all his defects. To the grave and formal Sir Lancelot—notwithstanding some amount of natural affection, which had developed itself when his son was an innocent child, but which had cooled considerably before the youth had advanced far into his teens—he was a "horsey," fast, "slangy" young man, in whom he tried in vain to discover any virtues that were sufficient to counterbalance his vices, and keep the scales from going down too unmistakably on the wrong side.

III.   11

To Lady Wyld he was in his young manhood what he had been in his infancy, the jewel of her heart, a creature all perfection because he was hers. A goose by nature, he was to her mind a beautiful swan, if not a very angel; because—and for no other reason than that—he had come into her household like a gift from Heaven, and she was his mother.

But her husband, knowing far better than a woman the impulses of young men's hearts, saw neither the angel nor the swan, but only the goose, in his son's character, and came to the conclusion that Lancelot's business in England had nothing to do with business properly so called, but that he had left America on account of the magnetic attraction of Patty Tidy. And Sir Lancelot was right, for if it had not been for thoughts of Patty and his vehement desire to see her again, all his other business might have been transacted by letter.

It was true, as Lancelot had written, that he liked America, that he was willing to pass the

remainder of his days there, that the life of a
planter and horse-breeder was congenial to his
tastes, that he saw his way to independence if
not to fortune in the new land, and that he
could be very happy there if he had but a wife,
and if that wife were Patty Tidy.

But he did not visit England without having
previously prepared the faithful Patty to receive
him.   He would have asked her to meet him at
Liverpool on the arrival of the steamer, except
for his conviction that she would not commit
such a breach of the proprieties.   He resolved,
nevertheless, that he would see her if possible
before he presented himself at the Rectory, but
how he was to manage the interview he could
not imagine.

It was for her sake that he crossed the
Atlantic, and he firmly made up his mind that
he would not cross it again, except in her
company.

Her letters were kind and tender, not always
correctly spelled or thoroughly grammatical;

11 *

but what cared he for grammar or orthography, if Patty did but let him know in her own way that she cared for him above all men in the world? And she did let him know this as eloquently as she could, and he believed her. Otherwise he would not have left America, for he was not particularly anxious to meet any of his racing creditors, or to be brow-beaten, reprimanded, and preached at by his father, though he would have been glad to have been once again by the side of his mother.

The young man had really taken a liking to the rough, democratic life of America, and thought that Virginia would be as much like Paradise as any spot of the world could be, if Patty were in it, and he had a stud farm with a few score of horses to make money of.

He really thought the rearing of horses was a more delightful pursuit than betting about them ; not that he could avoid, or did not love, betting. There was not the slightest thing in the world of which there was a doubt that he would not have taken the odds about if he could find anybody to bet with him. Betting was a part of his nature as the marrow was of his bones.

"I bet you," he said to himself, "that Patty will be glad to see me when I arrive in England. What's the odds? Two to one?—three to one? A thousand to one, by Jove!" And he was greatly satisfied with the thought, and as greatly dissatisfied that there was nobody with whom he could do business on that footing.

Patty's objections to marrying him were partly if not wholly removed by his promise to take her to America. Patty knew—as what pretty girl does not?—that she was a very attractive young person, and she was proud to have made a conquest of a Baronet's son, and in the thought that she too might in after time be called "my Lady."

But she did not care to become Lancelot's wife if she were to continue to live in her native Braxford, envied and perhaps hated by every girl in the village, besides being looked down upon by her husband's family, especially by that dreadful and severe Sir Lancelot, of whom she stood in great awe. And she thought at the same time that her father, of whom she was very fond, and whom she would not willingly displease, would possibly not be offended at her union with a prosperous farmer in America.

As Lancelot had promised to write to her from America, and as she did not care to be cross-questioned at home about her letters, she had made a *confidante* of Mrs. Bobbles, the postmistress of Braxford, and arranged with that motherly and inquisitive old woman—who had daughters of her own who had married and left her—that all letters addressed to her from America should remain at the Post Office till called for, and should by no manner of means be delivered at the smithy.

In this way the correspondence continued unsuspected; but as soon as she learned that Lancelot was coming home, and that his object in returning was to make her his wife, she thought it prudent to prepare her father and mother for the event.

Patty was a good girl, and a sensible girl; and though she had been somewhat of a flirt, and, perhaps, over fond of admiration—as most if not all pretty girls are, whether they be the daughters of dukes or of blacksmiths—she came to the conclusion, after her parting with Lancelot, that her flirting days ought to come to an end, that she did not really care "a bit"—no, not "the least little bit"—for the young organist at the village church, or for the farmer's son, with the attentions of both of whom she had been more or less flattered, and which she had accepted as tributes to her beauty.

She took out of the little leather bag which she wore at her bosom the half sixpence which Lancelot had given her at their last meeting, and kissed it, a little action which, could Lancelot have known in mid-Atlantic—where the Cunard steamer was ploughing its way

through heavy and heaving billows towards
Liverpool with him and a hundred other
passengers on board—would have caused a
thrill of pleasure to circulate through all his
nerves and arteries.

When Patty had finally made up her mind
that her father ought to know of her engagement,
she was sorely puzzled to think how she should
broach the subject. She was inclined to think
that she ought to tell her mother first, and after
sleeping a night upon it, she resolved upon this
course.

"Mother," she said after breakfast, when
Tidy had gone down to the smithy, "do you
think father very much dislikes Mr. Lancelot,
and that he never could be brought to look
kindly upon him if Mr. Lancelot tried ever so
hard to make him do so?"

"I can't say," replied Mrs. Tidy, a buxom
woman of very comfortable bulk, and almost as
round and as rosy-cheeked as an apple: "though
I scarcely think he could ever like any young

man who did nothing but drink, and smoke, and gamble."

"Lancelot does not drink," said Patty; "and though he once used to bet upon horses, he has given it up. And as for smoking, he does not smoke very much, and there's no harm in a cigar."

"Nor for the matter of that in a pipe either, leastways, if a man doesn't smoke in the bed-room. But why do you ask?"

"Because Mr. Lancelot has asked me to marry him."

"Lor!" said her mother, opening her little eyes wide, and her large mouth still wider.

"And though I should like to marry him, I shouldn't like to offend father. And Lancelot is quite a reformed young man now, and works very hard. He grows tobacco, and rears horses in Virginia, and has a farm all his own, and ten times larger than any of the farms in the Fens."

"Lor'" said Mrs. Tidy once again, finding apparently no other word to express her amazement at the news, and her fears of what her husband might say to it.

"And I 've almost made up my mind to accept him; and indeed I have as good as accepted him, and he 's coming back to England to take me away with him."

"Oh lor, oh lor!" said Mrs. Tidy. "My dear, my dear, I cannot let you go to the other end of the world! If he would settle here, now, and be a proper young man as you say he is, that would be different." And the good woman covered her face with her chubby hands and sobbed aloud. And Patty, as she saw the tears trickling through her mother's fingers, put her arms round her neck and wept with her.

"Girls must marry some time," she said, soothingly. "And you yourself married, and left your mother and father; and if I marry, I must go where my husband takes me."

"Oh, but that is very different," replied Mrs. Tidy, uncovering her wet, plump face, and wiping the tears from her blue eyes. "And I wasn't in a hurry; and my mother was dead before I married, and my father did not particularly care about me, for there were five other girls besides me. But you are my only girl, Patty, and I cannot, cannot lose you! And I don't think your father will ever consent to it. Oh deary me! There's nothing but trouble everywhere. And I could have been so happy! Joe has left me, and now you're going. I can't bear it, I can't."

"But Joe is doing well, mother, in America. I had a letter from him, which I was afraid to show father, because it speaks of Lancelot. Lancelot has been the making of Joe. He paid his passage to America, to get him out of his trouble about the poaching, and has taken him by the hand in America, and given him work on the farm, and more than double the wages he ever could earn in England. And Joe is coming back with Lancelot to see you."

Mrs. Tidy's face brightened. There was a bonnie blink of a rainbow amid her tears as she said,

" Oh, Patty! is this quite true? "

Patty assured her it was quite true, and showed her the letter in which the news was conveyed.

Mrs. Tidy put on her spectacles and read it carefully twice over. This done, she suddenly said,

" I must show it to father. May I? Let us go together, Patty."

" Go by yourself, mother," replied Patty, " and I will mind the house. I hope father will be pleased."

" Pleased! I should think so! " And in her joy at the prospect of speedily seeing her son she forgot, for the time, that she might as speedily be deprived of the company of her daughter. She ran rather than walked to the smithy; and running, to a person of her bulk, was hard work, and might have distressed her at any other time, but did not in the least distress her at this.

Tom Tidy was in excellent humour, indeed

he generally was, whenever his opinions on theology and the Poor Laws were not opposed or
roughly called in question, and was glad to hear
so good an account of " Joe." Turning the
letter over after he had read it, he noticed that
there was no post-mark upon it.

"How did Patty get this?" he asked, with a
very perceptible frown. "It did not come through
the Post Office."

The letter did not say that Joe and Lancelot were coming to England together, or the
frown on Tom Tidy's face would have been
blacker than it was; for he was not quite satisfied that Joe should ever have been beholden to
Lancelot Wyld for any favour whatever.

"I don't know how the letter came," said
Mrs. Tidy; " but Patty will tell you, if you want
to know."

Mr. Tidy did want to know, and going home
with his wife, found Patty standing at the porch,
perplexed and anxious, and asked her the question point blank.

Patty answered point blank, thinking it the best way, as it doubtless was.

"It was inclosed in a letter from Lancelot to me."

"And do you mean to say, you disobedient hussy," said her father, "that you have been carrying on a correspondence with that young blackguard Wyld, whom I disapprove of, a scapegrace of a fellow that never will come to good?"

"He's not a blackguard, father, and he has come to good," said Patty, her bright eyes filling with tears, and her lips quivering with sorrow and anger. "He has got a large farm in America, and grows tobacco, and has got fifty or sixty horses; and he employs Joe, and is very kind to him, and is going to remain in America."

"I'm glad to hear it," replied Tom, wiping his ample brow as he sat down on the bench in the porch; "very glad to hear it. And I'm sure I don't wish the young man any harm, if he have really taken to work, and lives respectably and keeps out of bad company."

Patty put her hand upon her father's shoulder, and looked piteously into his face.

"Don't call him bad names, father. He's not bad, he has a good heart; and there's nothing in the world that would please him so much as to have a kind word from you. He's not the first young man in the world who's been foolish."

"But he's worse than foolish," said Tidy, in a softer tone. "But I don't exactly say that he's a fool. I dare say the lad has some brains, but he doesn't know how to use them."

"He does know how to use them," replied Patty, growing bold in her lover's defence. "He didn't know what to do with himself down here, and his father was always unjust to him. But he's got a large farm, and he wants a wife to help him to look after it."

"I dare say he'll get one," said Tidy. "Fetch me a mug of beer, lass."

Patty tripped lightly away to fetch it, for she thought her father's heart was softening a little, and that if she was ever to tell him the real state of the case between her and Lancelot, the time had come. She speedily returned with the ale, and, pouring it deftly from the jug into a glass, made it froth briskly. And as her father drank, she said,

" So you think Lancelot will get a wife?"

" Easily," replied her father, wiping the froth off his lips with the back of his hand. " The girls are in such confounded haste to get married now-a-days that any fool of a man can get a greater fool of a woman to accept him! "

" But," said Patty, "is the world worse now than it ever was? and is it very foolish in a young man who has a large farm, if he wants a little wife to look after the house? "

" Well," said Tidy, with another swig at the beer, " I *do* think the world is worse than it was. Men used not to smoke their senses away when I was young, nor ruin themselves by rascally stupid bets, and continually living among horses."

" But I mean about marrying," urged Patty.

"Well, I suppose the world was always in the same way of thinking about marriage, and that it has always been out of its wits on that subject."

"But are the birds out of their wits?" said Patty, filling a little more ale into the glass.

"You're a saucy little baggage," replied her father, somewhat discomfited in his argument—if argument it could be called—but still in the best of humours.

"But if Lancelot be really reformed, as I know he is, and if he have a large farm, as I know he has, and he asks *me* to marry him, and I am willing to take him, will you be very angry?"

"You may be as willing as you like," said her father; "but if you do take him, my anger will go the length of renouncing you for ever."

Patty's cheeks flushed, and then grew suddenly pale. The flush came from resentment, and a sense of injustice, the paleness came from sorrow and regret that her father should be so obstinate. She was tempted to make an undutiful reply, but tears prevented her from saying more than

"Oh father, father, you are very unkind to me."

She walked from the porch indoors, and laid herself down upon the sofa, giving vent to her outraged feelings by a succession of sobs, which went to her mother's heart.

Her kind-hearted mother carefully tended her till she restored her to comparative calm, by gentle words and expressions of hope that her father would yet relent, as soon as he saw that she really loved Lancelot and that Lancelot really loved her. The burly blacksmith walked back to the forge without entering into any further discussion with his women folk, and on the way encountered Sir Lancelot and Lady Wyld walking together towards the village The blacksmith touched his hat somewhat defiantly, as much as to say, "I don't think it consistent with my dignity to cut you, though otherwise I would gladly do so."

The Baronet returned the salute in his stiffest

manner, and the Baronet's wife, when Tidy was
out of hearing, said to her husband,

"What a fine-looking old man Tidy is.   His
head is quite a study for an artist."

" A pestilent heretic! A demagogue! " replied
Sir Lancelot."

" And what a very handsome girl his daughter
is! " continued the lady without heeding her husband's petulance, "the very ideal of an English
country lass of the better kind—lively, healthy,
joyous, and innocent-looking.   If I were a young
man, I think, if I were not engaged to someone
else, I should fall in love with her."

Sir Lancelot disliked this conversation exceed-
ingly, for he thought it meant approval of his
son's courtship of Patty. He could not deny that
Patty was all that his wife represented her to be;
but then she was the daughter of Tom Tidy, who
was not only a Radical and leveller, but who dared
to have opinions of his own about the cosmo-
gony of Moses, which were antagonistic to those
which he held himself, and which he was entitled

12 *

to hold as the parson of the parish and the chief man in it. Had Tidy been a Methodist, a Baptist, a Quaker, a Presbyterian, or a Roman Catholic, he would not have had such strong objections to him, but to a man who disbelieved in the literal accuracy of the Mosaic account of the Creation, he could entertain no feelings but those of hostility and aversion. That his wife should even hint approval of such a man and his daughter was gall and wormwood to him.

"I have no objection to the young woman," he went on to say, "but I have a great objection to my son having anything to do with her or her family."

Lady Wyld, so far from being angry with her son for falling in love with so fine a young woman, felt rather pleased than otherwise that he should have done so, and would possibly have been still better pleased if she had known .that the fine young woman looked favourably upon his suit. But she kept her thoughts to herself and dropped the discussion.

Had Patty known that she had a friend in
Lady Wyld she would have dried more rapidly
than she did, the tears that had come into
her eyes when her father had spoken so harshly
to her.

There were two men opposed to her union
with Lancelot, her own father and Lancelot's;
but could she have been certain that the two
mothers were not only not antagonistic but
friendly, she would have taken comfort.

Of one thing she was sure—her father loved
her ; and she thought he would not be too hard,
if, after Lancelot's reappearance in the village,
he saw reason to believe that he had abandoned
his idle habits, taken to hard work, and was
possessor of a large farm in America.

Patty was pledged to Lancelot; she had given
him her heart as well as her word, and she
trusted that fortune, somehow or other, would
make all things right.

She had been unsuccessful in her first attempt
to overcome her father's objections; but, though

repulsed, she was not defeated. She th determined to return to the charge, with her mother for an ally; and her mother was an ally with whose power she was well acquainted.

Tom Tidy was a strong man, physically, morally, and intellectually; but he had his weak points, as his daughter knew from daily observation, and one of those weak points was his vulnerability to his wife's tears.

He could resist her arguments, and flattered himself that as a logician, compared with her, he was a giant to a dwarf. But to see tears in her eyes was a sore trial to him. And then Patty had tears of her own, as she had just shown, and she could use them as very potent artillery when the occasion demanded. So, though she was disappointed, she was not despondent, and took her half sixpence once again from her bosom, and thought of the happy day, soon to arrive, when Lancelot should produce the other half, and claim the performance of her promise.

CHAPTER XI.

It was but six days after these little events had occurred at Braxford, when Lancelot Wyld and his trusty henchman, Joe Tidy, arrived at Liverpool and proceeded straight to Baggs's private hotel, in Hatfield Street, Strand. Baggs had been forewarned by telegram to receive them, and did the honours of his dingily grand hostelry in his accustomed fashion, never forgetting to keep a keen eye on the possible waste of the mustard.

Lancelot was dimly informed of the Ravelstone peerage case, but would not have been greatly interested even if he had known all about it.

Having nothing to detain him in London, he resolved to start on the morrow for Swinston and Braxford. He had some information to convey to his uncle at Swinston, and as it was on the way to Braxford, he resolved to stay there for a few hours before presenting himself at home. And he had a kind of a notion that Patty would be at Swinston on the very day and hour when *he* expected to arrive there. Perhaps—who knows? —because he had previously informed her that at such a day and at such an hour a train from London would be due, and in that train would be her brother Joe. There was no occasion to tell her that somebody else would be there also.

Patty duly communicated to her father all that was in the letter, and not a syllable more, and obtained his permission to go to Swinston to meet her brother.

Mrs. Tidy resolved to accompany her, an arrangement with which Patty was not wholly satisfied; but when her father also resolved to be of the party, her dissatisfaction assumed a more potent form, and she was more than half inclined to let her father and mother go without her, not choosing that any unfavourable eye should witness her meeting with her lover. But the blacksmith speedily changed his mind. He did not care to exhibit a too great eagerness to meet his runaway son, though he was quite willing that his wife and daughter - should be more effusive.

Under these circumstances, Patty was reconciled to her mother's company, imagining that the good woman would be too exclusively occupied with Joe to devote any attention to Lancelot. And besides, Lancelot's letter of advice said nothing of himself, and she was not going to take her mother into her confidence, being well content that Lancelot's appearance should be, or appear to be, a surprise. Artful Patty!

They entered the station a quarter of an hour before the arrival of the train; and it is difficult to say to which of the two women the *mauvais quart d'heure* appeared the most tedious.

The love of mothers for their sons is some-times great, like that of fathers for their daughters; but the love of young lovers in the bloom and hey-day of their passion surpasses that of children and parents. So Patty was doubtless more impatient than her mother at the slow progress of the lazy-footed time, that seemed to her to stretch the minutes into hours.

But the train arrived at last, and Lancelot Wyld, alone, stepped on to the platform, and catching sight of Patty without being aware of the presence of her mother, clasped her in his arms, utterly careless of public opinion, and of rumour, and of scandal, and of the many censorious voices that might repeat how the Baronet's son had kissed the blacksmith's daughter at the Railway Station.

Joe had not arrived, for he was afraid that the unpleasantness of the poaching business had not quite blown over, and thought it would be more prudent to keep in the quiet solitudes of multitudinous London, where nobody knew or cared about him, than to show himself in Braxford, where he was as well known as the church-steeple or the parish pump.

Lancelot, after having paid his first warm homage to Patty, explained to Mrs. Tidy the reasons of her son's non-arrival, and conveyed to her an invitation from that young man to come and see him in London at Baggs's Hotel. The poor woman was much disappointed, and hastily resolved that she would go to London the very next day, and, if possible, take her husband along with her. Meanwhile, she could not help noticing how much more robust and handsome Mr. Lancelot had grown since he had been in America, and what a fine young man he looked.

"Tom (her husband) is too hard upon him," she thought, "and I don't see why, if he wants to marry Patty, he shouldn't do so. Patty's a fine girl, and he might go much further and fare worse."

And while this thought was passing through her mind, Lancelot confirmed the good impression he had created by insisting upon treating both mother and daughter to a glass of sherry in the Refreshment Room.

Mrs. Tidy demurred a little to the proposal, but she took the sherry and liked it, while Patty, in a perfect haze and whirl and dazzle of joy, drank but tasted not, knowing nothing, seeing nothing, feeling nothing, but that she was in Lancelot's presence.

"Change half-sixpences with me," whispered Lancelot, so that Mrs. Tidy should not hear.

Patty drew her half-sixpence from her bosom, but Lancelot more prosaically drew his from his purse, and the exchange was effected. They were both happy. The fast young man, and the innocent country girl felt the same electric throb, unaccountable, but all-pervading, when love, or what men call love, which is possibly nothing more nor less than electricity, travels along the nerves of the young and susceptible.

" Lancelot took a first-class ticket to Braxford.
Mrs. Tidy and her daughter took a third, as
it was thought advisible both by Lancelot and
Patty that there should be no close approxima-
tion in their travelling, lest the ill-natured, who
are the majority, should take notice of their com-
panionship, and comment upon it unfavourably.

Tom Tidy, though somewhat disappointed at
the non-arrival of his son, thought, on cool reflection, that it was just as well that Joe should not
appear in Braxford. The poaching affray had
become almost, if not quite forgotten, in the
neighbourhood, yet there might be ill-natured
people about, who might find a malicious pleasure
in reviving a scandal. So he rather liked his son's
prudence, in avoiding occasion for the wagging
of evil tongues, and resolved to accompany his
wife to London, and see the returned prodigal.

Lancelot called upon his uncle, at Mill Haughton, and saw that gentleman as well as Mrs.
Haughton and her daughters. He had news to
communicate which interested them all.   He

had returned from Virginia by way of Chicago
and the Great Lakes, in order that he might
take a look at Canada, and study its capabilities
for profitable agriculture.   He rested at Chicago
for a couple of days, before proceeding to
Quebec to meet the Liverpool steamer, and
on the second day was spectator of a very
mournful catastrophe.

A large lake steamer, of frail build, and
laden with about four hundred passengers,
had come into collision in the early morning
with a heavy fishing boat, and received such
damage that she went down bodily in less than
ten minutes. A terrific thunder-storm was
raging at the time with a violence seldom witnessed in the calmer latitudes of England, and
in the very height and fury of the tempest,
while flashes of lightning shot athwart the sky
with bewildering rapidity, the helpless passengers
and crew were cast into the water. There had
been a ball, or as the Americans call it a "hop,"
on board, for the amusement of the ladies and the

young people, which had scarcely ended before the storm began, and neither ladies nor gentlemen had had time to doff their ball-room finery before the fatal crash occurred.

The fishing boat was enabled to rescue a few of the passengers, and a few more managed to cling to the masts and planks of the broken steamer, and take their chance of drifting to shore, the rain raining, the thunder roaring, and the lightning flashing above their defenceless heads, as they struggled for life amid the uproar of the elements. The great majority perished in the waves, and hundreds, perhaps thousands of the population of Chicago turned out of their beds and proceeded to the shore, to render assistance to any survivors who might arrive in boats or on planks of the wrecked vessel. A few were saved, half-drowned, and restored to consciousness and life by care and attention.

The body of one man, whom Lancelot recognised at first glance, came to shore five hours after the fatal collision, with his arm around a spar of the steamer, to which he had clung amid the blinding storm for all that time. The body was still warm, and every means were adopted to restore him to consciousness and life, but all in vain. It was no other than that of John Rigglesby, late M.P. for Kilmacnoise, whose supposed suicide in London had excited so much wonder and scandal, and spread such misery among the duped depositors and shareholders of the Bank of which he was the Managing Director.

" Are you sure, positively sure, it was Rigglesby ? " asked Mr. Haughton.

" Positively sure," replied Lancelot; "and I recognised not only his features, but the right hand with the missing finger."

" What a dreadful death for a man who had such a nervous horror of lightning! You remember," he added, turning to his wife, " the scene we had with him in Iona? "

" Perfectly ; and it minded me o' the old saying that thunder was the voice o' God speaking to the wicked."

" And to suffer all that for five hours," said Euphemia, " doing battle with the waves for his life all the time. What thoughts must have passed through his mind, if merciful insensibility did not come to his aid! "

" In the breast-pocket of his coat," continued Lancelot, " were found some packets tied with red tape and closely sealed. One of them was addressed to ' Archibald Haughton, Esq., M.P., England,' and another to ' Lord O'Monaghan, England.' All the documents were taken possession of by the authorities at Chicago, and will, I suppose be given up to those entitled to claim them. It appeared from a card-case found in his pocket with cards in it that he passed in America under the name of Russell O'Dougherty, and that he resided in New York."

" Did you divulge the secret to the Chicago people ? "

" No, I didn't ; for I thought, by Jove ! that if I meddled in the business I might be detained to give evidence. That didn't suit my book, you know."

" Wasn't it awfully strange, the whole thing?" said Ettie.

" For once," said her father, "you have used the word ' awfully ' in a proper sense. It was indeed awful."

" I told the sheriff—I think they called him so—who took possession of Mr. O'Dougherty's papers that I was acquainted with Mr. Archibald Haughton, M.P., to whom one of the packets was addressed, and suggested that I should take care of it for you. But the sheriff did not see his way to trust me in the matter, and talked of forwarding them to you by post."

" Very proper on the sheriff's part," replied Mr. Haughton; "for how could he know that you might not be an impostor ? "

" I forgot to say that the corpse had a valuable diamond ring on the third finger of the left hand, worth, the sheriff said, at least a thousand dollars, and that a small jewel-case containing diamonds,

emeralds, rubies, and opals, valued at a considerable sum, were also found upon him, and
that they remain in the possession of the
authorities."

"The property, no doubt, of the unlucky
shareholders of the Bank that he robbed, and
of me among the number," remarked Mr.
Haughton.

Mr. Haughton was at first somewhat surprised
to see Lancelot back again in England, but was
pleased to be informed that he intended to
return immediately, that he liked the country,
and had taken not only kindly but eagerly to a
Virginian life, to its tobacco-growing, and, above
all, to the rearing of stock as well as of horses,
and that he had only come home to make some
arrangements with his father and mother relative
to his future life.

Lancelot did not mention a word of his love
affair. As he had no further news to communicate, he stayed to lunch with the family,
and then took his departure for Braxford, leaving

13 *

behind him in the minds of his uncle and aunt and two cousins a more favourable impression than they had ever formed of him before.

The remnant of horsiness that still clung to him, though greatly softened by his absence from the company of the professional betting men of London, with whom he had been accustomed to associate, was agreeable rather than otherwise to Miss Esther, who declared to her mother that she thought him particularly "nice," and that, in her opinion, it was an "immense" pity that he was not going to remain in England.

Lancelot's welcome to Braxford was, on the part of his mother, cordial in the extreme, and on that of his father not unkind, but, on the contrary, as kind as the Baronet's slow and tepid nature allowed, especially when he noticed with a critical eye that his son had lost much of the ancient manners of the stable, that he did not smell of rotten straw or stale tobacco, or use too much of the phraseology of grooms and jockeys.

Lancelot explained to them both what he wished them to consider the main reason of his sudden return to England—he did not say it was the only reason, though he was content that they should think so—and that reason was that he wanted to borrow money.

Sir Lancelot started, not very violently, but very perceptibly, and a frown stole over his face and darkened his eyes, till they looked what the Scotch, with a more admirable word than the English language yet possesses, call "drumlie."

His son went on to explain that the rate of interest in Virginia was eight, nine, and ten per cent.; that he wanted five thousand pounds, and thought he could raise that sum in England at five per cent., if the security were good.

Sir Lancelot was decidedly of that opinion, and that his son's preference of five per cent. to eight, nine or ten argued at least common sense and a dawning appreciation of real business.

"There is," continued Lancelot, "an estate of more than four thousand acres of fine land, with a good house and outbuildings, belonging to my cousin, near Petersburg; and my cousin, who has taken hold of me and taught me tobacco-raising and stock-rearing, wants to raise that sum in order to develop the resources of the estate, pay off encumbrances, and hire labour. He proposes to go into partnership with me, share and share alike, and I think the bargain a jolly good one. In short, it is dirt cheap. The disgusting Civil War has ruined one half of the gentlemen of Virginia, and our cousin nearly—not quite. I know that you only receive three per cent. for your money. We will give you five on five thousand pounds, and assign the estate to you as security. Is not that good business, mamma?" said Lancelot, who loved his mother with enough of boyishness of heart to object to the more formal word "mother," which is oftener used by the lower than by the upper classes; "and if you will lend it to us, it will be the making of me, and we shall be able to pay you back the principal in seven years."

Lady Wyld was surprised at the cool and sensible manner of her son in making this proposal, and Sir Lancelot began to perceive for the first time that his son was not without brains.

He was pleased also to note that Lancelot took so kindly to business, and that he felt inclined to abandon betting and gambling.

"It is all very well, Lancelot," he said, "if we can be sure of two things—first, that the land and its capabilities are as you describe them, and that the security is ample enough to leave a margin for eventualities in case of accident or bad seasons; and secondly, that you are steady enough and have knowledge and experience enough of your new business to work it profitably."

"Now don't, Sir Lancelot," said Lady Wyld, "begin to make objections; though I must say I don't altogether like the idea of Lancie's remaining in America for ever. Why can't he take a farm in England, and work here, instead of going so far away?"

" There is no such chance to be got in England," replied Lancelot. " Fifty, or even a hundred thousand pounds would not purchase such
a place in the Fens as the place in Virginia.
And then, you know, America is not so very
far off. The steamers cross in ten or eleven
days, and I can always get away for three months
in the winter, to come down and see your dear
old face in England, by Jove! "

Lady Wyld's "dear old face" lit up joyously
as her son spoke.

" Yes, Lancie, and I and your father, or I by
myself, if he won't accompany me, can come
over to Virginia for another three months for a
change. For Braxford is a dull place to stay in
during a whole year; you will confess as much
as that, Sir Lancelot, won't you?"

Sir Lancelot did not wish to confess. He
had his parochial and spiritual duties to perform.
Not that he really objected to visiting America.
But then there were two currents in his feelings,
the upper one being that his wife was spoiling

his son by her over-fondness, and that if he went
to America with her, merely to see Lancelot, it
would only tend to encourage her in her weakness.

"Well," replied Sir Lancelot, "Braxford *is*
rather dull, but it's the post of duty, and I must
remain at it. Nevertheless, I won't say that I
shall not go to America, say next year, if we
live so long. But it is time enough to discuss
the subject—it is not really before us at present.
The question is as to these five thousand pounds
—a very large sum of money, Lady Wyld, and
not to be parted with to a young man like
Lancelot without fuller knowledge and inquiry."

"Of course," replied his son, "the fuller the
knowledge, and the more careful the inquiry, the
better satisfied you will be of the truth of what
I say, and the more satisfied I will be—yes, by
Jove, I mean it!"

And Lancelot did mean it, though there was,
as his father thought, no necessity why he should
call "Jove" to witness it. Lancelot was skilled
in making a "book" for the Derby, and had

profited by that evil knowledge so far as to be aware that in a case of this kind documentary evidence was essential to a satisfactory transaction of business, and had come provided with all the legal proof of the existence and ownership of the estate of Blenheim, in Virginia, originally given to it by its first proprietor, a man of the name of Churchill.   For the Americans of English and Scottish descent cling fondly to the traditions and names of the old country, and the Camerons love to call their American homes "Lochiel," and the Stewarts delight in dwelling in Appin or Ardgowan.   Lancelot also produced a map of the estate and surrounding district, together with a power of attorney to raise money upon the security of the absolute fee simple.

He did not know how much he had raised himself in his father's estimation by the method and regularity of his proceedings, and what a triumph of his mother over his father he had aided that fond lady to achieve.   It will be sufficient in this place to state that after the

requisite—or rather the non-requisite—legal
delays—and punctilios and extra-punctilios, and
word-splitting and extra-word-splitting, and am-
plifications and extra-amplifications, and pro-
visos and extra-provisos—the matter was finally
arranged by Mr. Octavius Little, of Swinston, the
respectable and trusted solicitor of Swinston,
with whom the reader is already acquainted.

Lancelot's other business sped equally well.
His meetings with Patty were unobserved,
except by the busybodies of the village,
experts all of them at seeing through mill-
stones, above mill-stones, below mill-stones, and
all round mill-stones, and at converting the
shadows that they discovered into very palpable
realities. These busybodies, in the absence of
Tom Tidy and his spouse in London on a visit
to their truant son, knew how frequently, how
much too frequently, in fact, Lancelot and
Patty were to be seen at evening, under the
elms by moonlight or starlight. Some drew the
conclusion that marriage or something worse was

imminent, while many more were of opinion that
the something worse was far more likely to happen
than marriage.   But then the majority are generally wrong, because they are either ignorant,
ill-natured, idle, or indifferent, and act upon the
maxim jestingly put forward by Douglas Jerrold,
that if you don't know the rights of a thing it
is your duty to believe the worst.   Leaving
Lancelot and Patty to their pleasant devices,
unsupervised by Tom Tidy, though not wholly
unsuspected, or even wholly unseen by the Rev.
Sir Lancelot, we must accompany the sturdy
blacksmith and his wife to London.

Joe Tidy is not installed at Baggs's in the
grand, dark, dusty, magnificent, dreary first
floor, reserved for guests of more than ordinary
wealth or importance, but in an airy little room
on the fourth floor of the big house.

Tom Tidy has tolerably good wind still left in
him, but his buxom (and pursy) spouse com-
plains of the woful ascent, and has to rest at
each floor.   But as her son comes down to help

and escort her, the pair arrive at the summit at
last, where Tom Tidy finds a capacious jug of
ale ready for him, ale that only requires to be
poured into a tumbler from a sufficient height
to sparkle as if it were champagne.

Tom partakes, and Mrs. Tidy, after a little—
but very little—pressing, partakes also, and the
family consultation, preparatory to a substantial
dinner which Baggs has undertaken to provide,
is commenced and continued.

Mr. Tidy learns that his son is doing well in
Virginia, and is likely to do better under the
auspices of Mr. Lancelot, in his grand farm at
Blenheim. He also learns that Lancelot has
taken to hard work, and seems to like it.

Mr. Tidy is pleased to hear it, and acknow-
ledges in his own mind that he had no particular
objection to the young man, except the idleness
of the life he led in Braxford, and the court he
paid to Patty, which he disliked more on account
of Sir Lancelot than of his son.

The old man was particularly anxious to

learn the social condition of the Americans, and whether they were as pleased as he thought they ought to be with the democratic equality which every man enjoyed with every other, and in the absence of a titled aristocracy and the non-existence of any Game Laws.

"I like a country," he said, "where there are no Majesties, or Royal Highnesses, or Your Graces, or Your Lordships, and all that sort of trumpery, where ribbons, and stars and garters, and all that rubbish and tomfoolery, is left to the ladies."

"Well, I can't say," replied Joe, "as how I ever thought much about it; but I know that the Americans, as far as I have seen, are mighty fond of titles. Almost every man you meet is a General, a Colonel, a Judge, a Governor, or an Honourable, or something of that kind. What pleases me is that a man can shoot any game he likes, where he likes, and when he likes, and that there are no stuck-up Squires and Justices of the Peace to ruin a fellow's prospects for life for snaring a hare or killing a partridge, and all that downright tyranny as poor men have to suffer in England. Them's my opinions."

"Well, Joe," said his father, "I think if I were as young as you are, I should like to leave England and possess land of my own in America —out in the West, and not among the niggers, whom I can't bear."

"I thought," replied Joe, who saw a weak point in his father's admiration for democratic equality, "that you was of opinion that all men was alike, and that a black fellow was as good as a white fellow."

"I never said so; I never thought so," replied Tom Tidy. "You might as well ask me to agree that a donkey is as good as a horse. No, no! none of that for me. The doctrine may suit the preachers and the women over here, where you don't see a black man once in a twelvemonth; but in America, in the South, where blacks are more plentiful than whites, as

I 've heard, it won't answer. I wouldn't make slaves of 'em ; oh no! but hang it all! I wouldn't eat and drink with them."

"That's about the feeling in America," replied Joe; "though I know some niggers that are main good fellows, and do their work right well, that is to say, if you look after them. They wants looking after, and I think they likes to be governed by white men. They don't do much good when left to themselves."

"Well," added his father, taking another swig at the tankard, "as I said just now, I wouldn't mind making my home in America if I were a little younger."

Joe did not see the force of this remark.

"You can't be younger than you are, father; neither can I, or anybody. But you 're not a bit too old. Why, you 're only fifty-five."

"About that," replied Tom, "though my head looks older, on account of the snow on it, you see; but I 'm young in the arms and legs, and I think my heart, somehow, is younger still."

And Tom was pleased at the idea that he was only midway between the sunny side of sixty and the shady side of fifty.

"I wish you and mother would come over," said Joe.

"Oh deary me, no!" said Mrs. Tidy. "I couldn't abear to leave England."

"You'd have to 'abear' it, old woman," said her husband, "if I arranged it. If I went you wouldn't stay behind, would you?"

"Oh deary me, no!" she said again. "'Where thou goest I will go,' as the Bible has it; but were're both too old."

"Why, you're a young woman, buxom and hearty!" said the blacksmith. "Wouldn't you like to be the mistress of a farm of a thousand acres, now?—not as a tenant, you know, paying rent to the Duke of This or to the Marquis of T'other, but owning the freehold? By the bye, what's the price of land by the acre where you are, Joe?"

Joe scratched his head as if dubious.

"Well, you see, there's good land and bad land. Land that has to be cleared of the timber, and that ain't too cheap at three dollars an acre ; and land in the swamps that's good for nought; and land that was cleared a hundred years ago, and will grow anything, from tobacco to pumpkins, let alone Indian corn and buckwheat—you might get such land now at a bargain, for about ten dollars an acre, provided it warn't very close to a big city. But a man wants a wife, you see, if he buys land in America."

"Yes, no doubt," said his father, "and I've got one."

"But I haven't," replied Joe; "and I should like to take one out with me. There's Matilda Jennings, who used to live at the Rectory as lady's-maid, you know. Is she there still, or is she married?"

"She's there still," said Mrs. Tidy, "and not married; and what about her?"

"Only that I should like to marry her, that's all ; and take her out to America, if she'd go."

Tom Tidy was in a good humour, and did not
expect that his son would ever marry a lady, or
appreciate her after marriage if he did, and saw
no particular objection to this particular young
person.

"But didn't she refuse you once?" he asked.

"She did; and she didn't! She flirted with a
little, mean, dirty, contemptible slip of a grocer's
boy, and I was vexed, and I told her so. And she
was vexed at me, and we quarrelled. But we
should have made it up long ago if I hadn't
been obliged to leave Braxford about that poaching business. And as for the precious little snob
of a grocer's boy, I'd like to punch his head!"

The blacksmith did not say a word about
Patty, until Joe expressed his sorrow that she
had not come to London with them, and then
he said somewhat sharply,

"Tell me the truth, Joe, for I'm sure you
know all about it. Is young Mr. Lancelot Wyld
after her? and, if he is, what does he mean by
it?"

14 *

"He *is* after her," replied Joe, "and he
means to marry her if she'll have him. And I
wish she would, for she'd marry one of the best
fellows in all the world, a fellow as does not look
down at another fellow or give him the cold
shoulder because he is down—as most people
do—but helps him to get up again—as most
people don't. He's as good as gold, and a
thousand times better!"

Tom Tidy recognised his son's right and duty
to speak well of his benefactor, and said not
another word, either good or bad, about Lancelot
and Patty. This silence seemed to Joe to be
of good omen, as well as the silence that his
father had preserved in the matter of Matilda
Jennings.

The blacksmith remained a couple of nights
in London, and took "the old woman," as he
called her, to the play twice. He expressed
himself on both occasions as rather scandalised
at what he thought the unnecessary display of
young women's legs upon the stage, and at the

brazen "imperence" of the said young women, an opinion in which "the old woman" thoroughly coincided.

Before parting with Joe on his return, the blacksmith tried hard to persuade him to come down to Braxford; but Joe, while promising that he would think of it, dreaded the revival of the poaching scandal, and refused for the present, though he said he should dearly like to have a look at Patty.

He thought he would like to see Matilda Jennings also, but did not let the thought travel as far as his lips. It was ultimately arranged that in a few days Mrs. Tidy should return to London and bring Patty along with her.

CHAPTER XII.

BEFORE tracing the further course of the love affairs of Lancelot and Patty, of Joe Tidy and Matilda Jennings, a few words must be said about Oscar Lebrun, the new Lord of Ravelstone, not yet acknowledged by, or even presented to, the world under that title.

He was still Oscar Lebrun to himself, and to everybody but the Haughton family and their connections, and under the old name of Oscar Lebrun he resolved, as already stated, to go to Bordeaux to present himself to his mother, before finally entering upon a sphere of more exalted duty than he had ever before occupied.

The victorious Germans were besieging Paris, and the surest way to reach Bordeaux was to travel by sea. But Oscar postponed his journey from day to day, greatly to the joy of Euphemia, with whom he maintained a morning and an evening correspondence, as young and ardent lovers will, always finding something to say, which something, if not very greatly to their mutual edification, was very greatly to their mutual delight.

Oscar finally decided that it would be advisable to postpone his visit to Margaux until after his marriage, by which time he hoped that the siege of Paris would be raised, that peace would be restored to unhappy France, and that he might pass with his wife a pleasant autumn among the vines of his maternal ancestors.

Occasional visits to Swinston for a week at a time to transact business with Mr. Octavius Little, personally rather than by letter, were pleasant episodes in his life, which would have been one of unclouded serenity and brightness, had it not been for the repetition of the anonymous threats that had previously annoyed him, and formed the only clouds in the clear sky of his happiness.

He burned several of these documents in contempt, perhaps in disgust; but it dawned upon his mind at last that it was unwise to destroy them, and that, if it became imperative for his own comfort to put a stop to the annoyance by the prosecution of the offenders, the letters might prove useful in the hands of the police.

He told Euphemia and the members of the Haughton family nothing of this, but deemed it necessary for his own protection that he should not appear in the streets unarmed, and carried, not only a sword-stick in his hand when he walked abroad, but a six-chambered revolver in his pocket.

But these things, after all, were but slight ripples on the stream of his life, and alternating between London and Swinston, and always in

anticipation of the happy day when Euphemia
Haughton was to be his for ever, with the good
will of all her family, his days, like those of
Thalaba, " flowed happily by."

Lancelot Wyld, to use his own phrase,
" meant business " in returning to England—
the business of purchasing a share in the Virginian estate of his cousin Hiram, and the great
and paramount business of marrying Patty.
The first business was speedily put in course of
arrangement.   It pleased his mother, did not
displease his father, and seemed, the more it was
investigated, to recommend itself to the favourable consideration of all concerned.   The business of Patty was not to be so easily settled,
though the two principal parties were quite
agreed upon the subject.   Lancelot was still at
Braxford, and growing daily in the good graces
of his father by the soberness of his life, and the
marked change for the better that had taken
place in his habits and conversation, when it
became known in the village that Patty had

left home on a visit to London, and that she was likely to be absent for some days. Sir Lancelot and Lady Wyld, if they heard the gossip, never imagined that it could in any way interest or affect them. The villagers never suspected, but Lancelot knew, that she had gone to London to see her brother Joe, and for another purpose, infinitely more important to herself, and to one other person in the world. She had been gone two days, during which time neither her name nor that of her father had been mentioned in the Rectory, when Lancelot announced his intention of proceeding to London to meet the solicitor of his cousin Hiram, and confer on the matter of the mortgage on the Virginian estate.

Lady Wyld raised no objection; how could she, as a sensible woman? and Sir Lancelot raised none, for he was a sensible man, and thought he thoroughly understood the management of affairs. But though Lancelot divulged part of his intentions, he did not think it prudent to divulge the whole of them, for fear of accident, interruption,

or interference, neither of which was likely while
he kept his own counsel.   So he freely divulged
ten per cent. of his intentions to Lady Wyld and
his father, that ten per cent. being quite sufficient
to satisfy them as to the legitimacy of his London
journey, and kept ninety per cent. safe in the
custody of his own heart.

On arriving in Hatfield Street, he commissioned
Joe, who had been forewarned of his coming, to
mount to the fourth floor of Baggs's hostelry,
and ascertain whether his old acquaintance Mr.
Scump, the racing prophet and sporting reporter,
was within.

"There is no need to look for him," replied
Joe.   "He went out early in the morning, and
told me he would be sure to see you before he
went to bed."

"All right," replied Lancelot.   "Have you
engaged a carriage and pair for eleven o'clock
to-morrow? and have you told Scump of the
arrangement?"

"I 've done everything you told me."

" And does old Baggs suspect anything? "

" I don't know what he suspects, but he knows nothing."

" And Patty? Will she keep faith ? "

" She's all right enough," replied Joe, " she's rather scared like, and no great wonder! But she's good as gold, true as steel, and firm as a rock! She's got the blood of her father in her, and when she makes up her mind, her mind's made up, see if it isn't! "

" I should like to call upon her to-night," replied Lancelot.

" Then why don't you? " asked Joe. " I would if it were my case. If it was Matilda Jennings I wanted to see, I should like to know who or what would stop me, except it were Matilda herself. And I'm sure Patty wouldn't stop you."

It should have been recorded that Joe had taken lodgings for his sister at the other end of Hatfield Street for a week, of which three days had elapsed. As it is not usual for young men in

London to take lodgings for young women, it was necessary to explain to the landlady, a very worthy soul, who soon took a liking to the buxom young woman, that her brother had got into a difficulty at home, that he did not care to show himself in the country just at present, that his father and mother had come up to see him, and that she had done the same, so as to be able to bear him company for a few days, before he took his departure for America, never, perhaps, to return to England again. The explanation was entirely true, and the respectability of Hatfield Street, as represented by the landlady, was satisfied.

Lancelot was fully aware of the censoriousness of the world, and would give it no such opportunity of wagging its tongue against pretty Patty, as would, could, or might be afforded if he visited her alone. So he resolved to visit her that afternoon along with Joe, feeling assured that scandal, however vivacious, could have nothing to say under such circumstances. And scandal having nothing to say, said nothing, and Lancelot had the satisfaction—though Joe was present, and neither heard nor saw, or in other words, did not choose to hear and see—of giving to and receiving from Patty the kiss, or rather several kisses, of affianced lovers, and of satisfying himself that a certain agreement which they had made between themselves for the morrow forenoon, an agreement which involved the breaking of no commandment but the fifth, held good, and was not to be broken by the weaker vessel.

Lancelot and Scump that evening partook of some whiskey toddy together. Lancelot, not being a Scotsman, was not particularly partial to that beverage; but Scump, though no Scotsman, delighted in it, and Baggs brought them some " Campbelton," which, he affirmed on his honour, had been thirty years in the stone jar in which he served it up, and which he declared to be cheap at a guinea a bottle, but for which he would only charge double the price of common whiskey.

Lancelot thought the price rather "stiff"; but Scump not only thought it cheap, but that it was incumbent upon him to drink a good modicum of it while he had the chance. Scump's talk was all of races; Lancelot's talk was all of horses and the noble "strains" of Kentucky and Virginia.

"I tell you what, old man," he said; "I don't think I shall ever bet upon a horse again. Better to raise horses and sell them, as I am going to do, than bet and wager about them. I 've turned over a new leaf, you see, and Patty has made me do it."

"A woman is always the cause of some mischief or other," replied Scump; "but all I have to say is, what 's the odds as long as you 're happy? And I hope that a winner of the Derby may come out of your stables in America! Wouldn't it make a sensation if a Yankee horse were to win it?"

"The Virginians are not Yankees," said Lancelot, in the pride of his superior knowledge.

"If ever you go to America, don't you call a Virginian gentleman a Yankee, or you'll see snakes, I can tell you. By Jove! he'd put a bullet through your head in no time! However, that's neither here nor there. You'll breakfast with me at ten to-morrow, and be ready to start at eleven."

"Honour bright!" said Scump. "I never failed a pal in a bad cause, and I'm not likely to fail him in a good one. So good night, old fellow."

That night Patty Tidy took her landlady, Mrs. Rammles, a little further into her confidence, and informed her that she was engaged to be married to the young gentleman who had accompanied her brother that afternoon, that he was the heir to a Baronetcy, that he would be rich some day, that he was her brother's very best friend, and that he was the kindest, best young man that ever lived.

"And does his family know about it?" asked Mrs. Rammles.

" Not altogether," replied Patty. " They know a little; not all."

" But are you sure, my dear," said Mrs. Rammles, "that his intentions are honourable, and that he really means to marry you?"

" Honourable!" ejaculated Patty, " of course they're honourable! And if he means to marry me! Why we're to be married to-morrow morning, Mrs. Rammles, and I want you to go with me, and be a witness of the ceremony."

"Oh Lord, oh Lord!" said Mrs. Rammles, almost gasping for breath. " And are you quite sure you are going to do right? Should not his family know? Do think a little."

" I have thought a great deal," replied Patty. "Lancelot has his witnesses ready, my brother Joe and an old friend. I must have at least one witness. Be that one, dear Mrs. Rammles!"

" Dear Mrs. Rammles," to whom a marriage, as it is to all women who are not too old and too stupid to be interested in the affairs of the world and the heart, was a thing of the highest

interest, consequence, and delight, made some
small and poor excuses, which she would have
been sorry to have had accepted, and finally
agreed to be a witness.

"But are there to be no bridesmaids, my
dear?" she inquired suddenly.

"No; no bridesmaids," replied Patty. "We
are to be married at the Registry Office."

"Oh dear! I don't like that," said Mrs.
Rammles. "Are you sure that the Registrar, as
you call him, can marry you as safe as a clergyman?"

"Oh, quite sure. My father says so; and he
knows everything, and is cleverer than the parson
of the parish. He always said he hoped I would
be married at a Registry Office. And Lancelot
wishes it to be so for the present. He pro-
mises me that we shall be married in church
afterwards, to make, as he calls it, 'double
sure,' and I 'm then to have as many bridesmaids
as I like, though I don't care about them,
jealous things! But meanwhile he doesn't want

any fuss; and why should I make a fuss, if he does not like it, especially if the marriage is good and binding, for ever and ever?"

Mrs. Rammles did not quite like the idea, but her curiosity to see a marriage at a Registry Office prevailed over her hesitation. The good lady was grand in her ideas, and her imagination prompted many of the supposed facts in her own career which she narrated to Patty.

"Ah, my dear," she said, "when I was married I had no less than twelve bridesmaids, all dressed alike, and looking like angels in their beautiful silk dresses, all trimmed with real lace, I do assure you. There was not one among them whose dress did not cost fifty guineas. And the ceremony was performed by a Bishop, assisted by three other clergymen."

Patty thought this was what Joe would have called a "crammer," and that if the truth were known, there was no Bishop, but only a curate, and perhaps no bridesmaids at all.

"What did the Bishop want assistance for?"

15 *

she inquired. " Couldn't he have performed the work alone ? "

" No doubt he could, if my husband wanted to do the thing cheap," said Mrs. Rammles; " but then mine was a real, real marriage, and very grand."

" And mine will be a real, real marriage," rejoined Patty; " and ten Bishops could not make it a bit more real than it will be. And as for a grand marriage, I don't care about it—that is, my husband that is to be does not care about it; and besides, it's not convenient, at least, just now."

At ten o' clock, attired in his best dress coat, with a rose in his button-hole, Scump appeared at the breakfast-table.

Lancelot was still more spruce, and radiant with joy and expectation.

Old Baggs, who, with Joe, waited at table, was at a loss to know what was going on, and made several side attempts to discover.

" Only a match, you know ! " said Scump;

"an event that's coming off. Something handsome to be won, you know."

"Yes," said Baggs, "and lost, I've no doubt. I thought Mr. Lancelot had given up horse-racing to please his father and Lady Wyld."

"Don't distress yourself, old fellow," said Scrump; "it's all right. Let us know the moment the carriage comes. Two splendid bays, fast goers, tip-top, the stylish thing, and no mistake!"

The carriage was punctual. Lancelot and Scump took their places inside, and Joe mounted on the box with the coachman, giving him directions where to drive. Baggs listened, but could not hear a word, and shut the street-door, disappointed.

Lancelot arrived first at the Registry Office, but only two minutes before Patty, accompanied by Mrs. Rammles, made her appearance—Patty blushing, beautiful, excited, and somewhat nervous; Mrs. Rammles nervous also, but visibly disappointed to observe the plain appearance of the office, and of the Registrar, who looked, as she afterwards declared, more like an attorney receiving instructions from a client than a functionary who had power to tie a man and woman together in the holy bands of matrimony. When the simple ceremony was over, and duly witnessed, the fees paid, and Patty Tidy legally transformed into Mrs. Lancelot Wyld, Scump and Joe, as by previous arrangement, accom·panied by Mrs. Rammles, took their departure for the Crystal Palace, to partake of a private dinner, with unlimited champagne, provided at the expense of Lancelot.

The bride and bridegroom, also by previous arrangement, lunched together at a fashionable restaurant in Regent Street, and afterwards drove to the terminus of the Great Northern Railway at King's Cross. Lancelot took an affectionate farewell of his bride.

"Patty," he said, "you're mine now, mine for ever. I'm the happiest fellow alive. Go home to your father and mother. Say nothing to

anybody. Keep your marriage certificate safe in
your bosom, my darling, along with that blessed
half-sixpence I gave you before I went to
America; and wait until I come and fetch you,
with flying colours, by Jove! and all the honours.
That five thousand pounds business well finished
and safe, you shall be mine as openly before
all the world, father and mother included, as
you are now secretly before God and the law!
God bless you, Patty!"

Patty wept hot tears—not of disappointment,
for she had known all along that this was to be
the arrangement, had agreed to it, and reconciled
herself to it—but tears of natural sorrow that she
was to be separated, even for a day or an hour,
from her so newly-made husband.

"It won't be for long, Patty. Perhaps for
not more than a week. And anyhow, I shall
be in Braxford the day after to-morrow; and
if I court you, as I did before, people will
think it's all right, and never know that I
am courting my wife, by Jove! Dry up your

tears, darling; and if ever again you have cause to shed any it shan't be my fault! Good-bye."

He ran alongside of the departing train the whole length of the platform, and saw, as long as the train was in sight, the fair face of his bride; and when that became invisible in the distance, the waving white handkerchief that—after the train was wholly lost from his view—was to be wet with the genuine tears of as good a little woman as the sun ever shone upon.

Lancelot was not given to tears himself—he thought himself too much of a man for that; but he felt a choking sensation in his throat, which he tried to relieve in the Refreshment Room by a draught of seltzer-water slightly flavoured with brandy. Next he lit a cigar, felt better, and drove quietly back to Baggs's. Before retiring to rest that evening, three additional cigars were necessary to his serenity of mind. When he tapped off the ashes of the first, he thought to himself that the "Governor" would be in an awful rage; and he hoped he would be, for then his mother would come to the rescue. As the second cigar was wearing to a stump he was of opinion that neither the anger of Sir Lancelot nor the calmer displeasure of his mother would last long. And by the time that he threw the end of his third cigar in the fireplace, he was satisfied that both of his parents would resign themselves to the irretrievable and irreparable—Sir Lancelot, perhaps, with a bad grace, but Lady Wyld with the good grace of a good heart that was not controlled in its working by a superabundant weight of worldly wisdom. And then he went to bed, and dreamed of Patty.

CHAPTER XIII.

IT was about a week after Patty's marriage—that still remained a profound secret, and not a suspicion of which had entered into the mind of anybody at Braxford—that a rumour was spread about the village that old Tom Tidy intended to leave England with all his family and settle in America.

How the rumour originated and whence it came nobody could tell. Rumours are like the thistle-down and other floating seeds that are planted by the wind and take root in unlikely places. Everybody in Braxford had heard this rumour, except Tidy himself, his wife and daughter.

When it reached the ears of the Rev. Sir

Lancelot Wyld and his wife, they both wondered whether it could possibly be true.

" I hope it is true," said Sir Lancelot at breakfast, " and that the parish will soon be rid of him."

" But is he not a very honest, industrious man ?" inquired Lady Wyld; "a substantial man, well to do in the world, and very much respected ? "

" Why, yes; he is all that," answered Sir Lancelot, with some hesitation, as if he were unwilling to confess so much; " and as soon as he leaves the parish, if he is going to leave it, I shall not have a word to say against him, and will cheerfully admit his many excellent qualities. A good, sturdy, honest, independent Englishman. If he had only believed in the Mosaic account of the Creation, and been my Churchwarden, I should have esteemed him as highly as any other man in the parish. But as it is, the less I say of him the better. Such men are dangerous in small communities, and teach their comrades to think wrong."

"But," said his lady, not quite sure that her husband was quite right in taking the Mosaic account of the Creation too literally, "is it not to his credit that he has the courage to think for himself, even if he does think wrong according to you, but right according to himself? Why are brains given to us unless we are to make use of them?"

"Very true," replied her husband; "but there is use and misuse. In Tidy's case it is a misuse; and then, all men's brains are not of equal power."

"But mightn't Tidy retort upon you, and say the misuse was on your side and not on his, and that his brains were as good as yours?"

"I don't think argumentation on theological subjects is edifying in ladies," replied her husband, not liking the turn the conversation had assumed, and taking up the newspaper as if he were going to read it again.

"That means," replied his wife, "that we ladies, as you call us, ought to believe all we are told."

It did mean that, in Sir Lancelot's mind, as far as theology was concerned; but he didn't like to say so in plain terms, so he made a diversion, and said,

" But after all, it may not be true that Tidy is going to emigrate. I wonder how the story originated? Going with his son, perhaps."

" Well," replied Lady Wyld, "if the case were so, Lancelot, who has been so good to his son, would probably know something about it, and if you are curious in the matter we can ask Lancelot on his return home to-morrow."

Lancelot *was* asked the question, and replied that Joe had strongly recommended his father to go to America, and that Tidy was only un-willing because he thought he was not young enough to try his fortune in a new country. This objection his son had endeavoured to over-rule, with what success Lancelot could not say. This was all the information in the power of Lancelot to bestow, and his father, meanwhile, was compelled to be satisfied with it.

If he had known that Lancelot had married the obnoxious man's daughter, and that possibly Tidy might feel inclined to remain in Braxford, standing in such relation to the Rev. Sir Lancelot, that the two might become grandfathers to a future inheritor of the baronetcy, the desire of Sir Lancelot for the emigration of Tidy might have been still more vehement than it was. However, as he knew nothing of this, his heart did not grieve about it.

The village gossips noticed that, since her return from London, Patty looked more than usually grave and staid, and did not associate with any of them so familiarly as before.

The elder women also remarked a change in her, a certain air of dignity and self-consciousness which they had not previously observed; while Harry Talmadge, the handsome young organist, who had never wholly lost hope of making an impression upon her, discovered that every attempt at a flirtation or even a civility on his part was received by Patty with a coldness that seemed to savour of aversion. And then he knew—as everybody in the village knew, except Tom Tidy and Sir Lancelot Wyld—that Patty took evening walks with Lancelot, and that the pair chose the most lonely spots for their meeting. So Harry Talmadge lost heart and hope, and caught himself more than once thinking or saying,

> "If she be not fair to me,
> What care I how fair she be?"

And he found comfort in the repetition of the words, and asked himself, like the hero of a more modern song,

> "Shall I for a hizzie dee?
> She may gang to France for me"

—or to some other region, for which France was the euphemism.

According to a previous agreement, Sir Lancelot and Lady Wyld, accompanied by Lancelot, went on a short visit to the Haughtons. Here Lancelot learned the romantic story of Oscar Lebrun, and of his once almost hopeless, but now happy attachment to Euphemia Haughton.

Lancelot thought to himself that if one "fellow" could be so fortunate in his love affairs, another "fellow" might be equally happy—not so much in the love itself, for in that respect he was as happy as a "fellow" could be, but in the acquiescence and good-will of his relatives. And a "fellow," he thought, need not be a newly-discovered Lord to get over difficulties of that kind.

He had got over the first great difficulty, and he expected that all the rest would be comparatively easy to surmount; and if not, he should be sorry, of course, but he shouldn't be inconsolable while Patty remained to him—Patty, that seemed to his eyes so infinitely more beautiful than either Effie or Ettie Haughton.

He thought, however, that his French cousin, whom he had never seen, was a lucky fellow, " by Jove!" to have secured such a prize as the

pensive, refined, and lovely Miss Effie.   As for
Miss Ettie, when he bestowed a thought on her,
he was of opinion that, if he had been a free
man himself, his choice would not have fallen on
one so self-confident.

Fast men don't like fast women; men who
talk slang don't seriously care about women
who imitate their example; and   the   most
devoted lover of smoking would be sorry to
link his fortunes with those of a woman who
smoked half as many cigars as himself, or who
smoked at all.

He learned that the lively Miss Esther had
two suitors, the Rev. Hope Smithers and Mr.
Barnard Strutt, Junior, to both of whom he
was introduced by Mrs. Haughton, and he took
odds with himself—there being nobody else to
take "odds" with him—that Mr. Barnard Strutt
would be the " winning horse," notwithstanding
the good looks, the fair, womanly hands, the
regular white teeth, the magnificent brown hair,
and the handsome " build " of the Rev. Hope

Smithers. And Lancelot judged that the Rev. Hope Smithers, who was poor, wanted the money, and that Mr. Barnard Strutt, who was rich, wanted the woman; and that if Miss Ettie discovered this, as she doubtless would in due time, the betting on Mr. Strutt, would be the safest " book " to make.

It will thus be seen that Lancelot still looked upon all things, or most things, from the point of view of Tattersall's and the race-course, and that the vocabulary of the stable was apt to introduce itself into his conversation.

Mr. Haughton had received from Chicago the packet addressed to himself which was found on the person of Mr. Russell O'Dougherty of New York, *alias* Mr. John Rigglesby, Member of the British Parliament, the news of whose tragical death in the waters of Lake Michigan had been brought to England by Lancelot.

The letter did not wholly clear up the mystery of the suicide on Blackheath, which had created so painful a sensation in London at the time of

its occurrence, though it threw some light upon
it. It was read aloud by Mr. Haughton to his
family and guests at the breakfast-table, and ran
as follows:

"I know not whether this letter will ever
reach the hands of him to whom it is addressed.
I have several times resolved to send it, but
have always invented reasons why I should
delay. I write, it may be in the performance
of a duty, or it may be only for the relief of
my mind. For three years before the final
catastrophe, and total ruin of my hopes and
fortunes, I led a life of daily misery. I appeared
to be great, to be powerful, to be rich, and I
was only great and powerful on the false pretence of riches that I did not possess.

"I had not a penny that was honestly my
own, and every day, or every hour, while I held
my head high in the world, and was supposed to
be a man whose favourable opinion and support
were passports to success in enterprises of magnitude, I lived in fear of disclosures that might

16 *

bring me face to face with the law, and stamp my name with infamy.

"I dwelt in this purgatory until I became old before my time, and every morning when I arose, after uneasy sleep, troubled with horrible dreams and nightmares, and looked at my face in the glass, I seriously debated whether it would not be better to draw the razor through my throat ; but I refrained, and lived on in the expectation of better fortune.

"I was thought to be a lucky man. People imagined that I had the gift of Midas, and that everything I touched would turn into gold. And so it did for a time, for the shares of every company to which I gave or sold my name as a Managing Director, even if they were at a discount, mounted up to a premium as soon as it became known that John Rigglesby had joined the undertaking.

"It was all a delusion and a snare, and the imagined Crœsus was as poor as a beggar. I came at last to look upon myself as a living lie, prompted by the Devil to deceive everybody, and take toll of the substance of widows and orphans.

"But I did not spend the gold on myself. I kept neither hounds, nor horses, nor yachts, nor theatres; neither did I give magnificent dinner parties to male fools, nor balls to female ones; or live but in the most frugal manner, taking my chop and my pint of claret at the Club, as if I were no richer than the confidential clerk of a great merchant.

"My ambition was to be at the head of a party in Parliament, and to aid the return of candidates who would look upon me as a leader, and follow me into the lobby on decisions of great moment, on which the fate of Ministries depended.

"I will not divulge the names of the Members of Parliament whose election expenses I paid, in whole or in part, and who acted the part of satellites to me, the central sun of the system. The cost was great, and the satisfaction small.

But, nevertheless, the game might have lasted much longer if it had not been for the frightfully unexpected collapse of a project, by the success of which I hoped to recover all previous losses. This brought about the final catastrophe.

" It was my intention, when I resigned my seat in Parliament, to commit suicide, and I left home for that purpose, disguised so that no man might know me. I hesitated between drowning and poisoning myself, for I hated the sight of blood too much to resort either to the razor or the pistol; but when the first furious paroxysm of my dread of coming shame had passed over, I resolved to live yet another day. I had a strange unwholesome curiosity to learn what the world would say of me, and whether one of the many friends on whom I had lavished my gold —that is to say, the gold of other people—would breathe a word of pity for my misfortunes, or in extenuation of my faults.

" On leaving home in the middle of the night, with my last ten sovereigns in my pocket, I walked from London to a small village in Surrey, about thirty miles distant, and feeling fatigued after the journey, paid for supper and a night's lodging at the little inn of the place, and slept more soundly than I had done for six months. I remained three days, unresolved whether to live or die; and the third morning, before preparing for another tramp for life or death, I saw in the London newspaper, that the host put before me while awaiting breakfast, that the dead body of a gentleman had been discovered on Blackheath, and that it was supposed from the dress and personal appearance to be that of John Rigglesby, late Member of Parliament for Kilmacnoise, whose mysterious disappearance from society had been the talk of the town ever since its occurrence. The announcement amused me in my misery, and I resolved to live until after the Coroner's inquest.

" It appeared that the unfortunate corpse had a very striking resemblance to myself, and that people with whom I had been more or less familiarly acquainted, agreed that it was the body of John Rigglesby, and of none other. The question of identity was ultimately left in doubt. It was not for me to clear it up.

" My resolution was soon taken. My disguise was ample, and I proceeded by rail to Liverpool, where I took a steerage passage by the first steamer for Quebec, which I thought a safer place for a while than New York. I have remained in America ever since, unsuspected, unknown, unlooked for, uncared for, though I have passed persons in the streets who once knew me, who seemed to look curiously at me for a moment. I have lived an idle and a miserable life all this time, and subsisted upon much less than the wages I formerly paid to my butler, derived from the sale of a few diamonds and rubies which I had purchased in the height of my seeming prosperity, with a view to the catastrophe that finally occurred. Life in a certain sense has long been odious to me, and yet I clung to it, simply, I suppose, because I have been too great a coward to die by my own hand. I don't know why I have selected you for my confidant, from among all the persons whom I have defrauded, unless it be that I have not ruined you, and that, being able to hold up your head in the world, maintain your high position, and reflect that you are able to look every man in the face and say that you owe him nothing, you may, from the calm heights of your superiority, pity, if you do not forgive me.

" Were it possible for me to make restitution to you and others, I would make it; but my poor diamonds would not pay a farthing in the pound of my indebtedness. And I have one wretched consolation in the extremity of my anguish, which is to think that if I have injured many, it was not from intention to injure, but from unwise reliance upon what I considered my ' luck,' and the delusion which always possessed me, that things would come right for me and everybody else, in what I called ' the long run.' Moreover, when I had money, honestly or dishonestly obtained, I never shut my heart (if ever I had one) or my purse against the claims of friends and acquaintances who were in extremity, or poorer than myself, and needed my assistance; not even against unknown strangers—possibly impostors—who appealed to my sympathies."

The body of the manuscript ended here, with the signature "J. R." Immediately afterwards there was appended the word "Postscript," as if the writer had intended to supplement his confessions by some particulars which he had inadvertently omitted. But no writing followed, except the one word "I." What the "I" would have said, remained a mystery which death had sealed up in this world for ever.

"The way of the transgressor is hard," said Sir Lancelot, when the reading was concluded, "and always is, and always will be, if we could see into men's hearts, as this erring sinner has enabled us to see into his."

"Puir body!" said Mrs. Haughton. "What he

must have suffered in the thunder and lightning!"

"Yes, indeed," added her husband. "If I had read this story in a novel I shouldn't have believed it."

"And what, I wonder, has become of his diamonds?" said Ettie.

"They'll be safe enough in the hands of the Chicago people," answered Lancelot, "until the rightful heirs come forward to claim them."

"The rightful heirs are his creditors, at least I take it to be so," said Mr. Haughton, "and I am one of them; but I would much rather abandon all my claims to the whole or any part of them, than spend a single sixpence in the attempt, probably a fruitless and certainly a very expensive one, to recover possession of them. Nevertheless, there are widows and orphans whom he has brought to distress if not to penury, who might be glad to receive back an instalment, however small, of the money they have lost through their confidence in this unhappy

bad man. And perhaps it will be better if a
meeting of the creditors were called, to decide
whether proceedings should be taken in the
American courts for the recovery of these value-
ables. I'll see Mr. Little on the subject, not in
my interest, but in theirs. As far as I am concerned the milk is spilt, and I shall waste no
time in the attempt to mop it up. I have been
taught a lesson by John Rigglesby, and I can
profit by it without being grateful to my
teacher."

And so the subject dropped.

CHAPTER XIV.

THE mortgage of five thousand pounds, in Lancelot's interest, on the freehold of the estate of Blenheim, in Virginia, was concluded with as few delays as legal necessity and rigid punctilio allowed, and Lancelot was at last in the position of being able to return to America, the money at command, and to commence operations on the fruitful farm, of which, thanks to his mother's kindness and trust in his honour and sagacity, he had become part proprietor.

As this business was arranged to the young man's satisfaction, Mr. Haughton thought the

time had come when he should be informed of
the liberality of old Mrs. Haughton, and the
payment by that high-minded and benevolent
lady of the debts of honour he had incurred in
his unlucky turf transactions.

"In all probability," said Mr. Haughton in
communicating the intelligence, "your grandmother would have left you the money in her
will; but she thought it better for the credit of
the family that these debts should be extinguished
in her lifetime, and that she should know the
fact—that they were extinguished. And, Lancelot, mark me well, you are bound to prove your
gratitude to her in the most unmistakable
manner."

" How can I ? oh, how can I ?" said Lancelot.
" Words cannot do it! "

" No!" rejoined his uncle. "She expects deeds
—negative deeds, not positive ones. She expects
that from henceforth you will never make a bet
on a horse, or on anything else."

" Never, upon my honour!" said Lancelot,

greatly affected. " Never! never, to the extent
of more than a 'fiver' ! "

" Better not at all, not even to the extent of
a farthing; and you must pledge your word to
her before you return to America."

A load of trouble was thus removed from
Lancelot's mind, and he felt more at ease
than he had ever done in his life. But
there still remained the awkward business
of Patty Tidy. Should he go off to Virginia
and take her with him, without explanation
to Sir Lancelot and Lady Wyld, and last,
not least, to Patty's father, who loved his
daughter as much as Jephtha, Judge of Israel,
loved his? Or should he and Patty make full
confession of what they had done, and trust
to the common sense of the old people to be
reconciled to the doing of a deed that none of
them could undo?

It was a difficult question for the young
people ; but Lancelot, who at first thought, to
use his own phraseology, that he would " hook

it with his wife," decided, on second thoughts, that it would be better to be fair, open, and above-board—to tell the whole truth and take all the consequences.

In pursuance of this resolution he presented himself, at the hour of noon, at Tidy's neat cottage, and found him, as he expected he would, sitting in the porch, in the shadow of the roses and honeysuckles which had been trained over the door, with his usual tankard of ale at his side, which his daughter had just brought him, fresh from the cellar.

Mrs. Tidy sat in the porch also, opposite to her husband, and Lancelot could not help thinking how comfortable they looked, a veritable *tableau vivant* of Darby and Joan, or "John Anderson my Joe," and his spouse, and what a pity it would be if what he was going to tell them should interrupt the tranquil current of their happiness.

Mr. Tidy's heart was softened towards the young man, not only because he knew that he had cast off the idleness that was once his prevailing vice, and the habit of horse-gambling which had grown out of it, but because Lancelot had been a good friend to his son Joe in the hour of need, and drawn him away from evil associations.

"Will you walk inside, Mr. Wyld?" he said, "or will you sit in the porch and taste my home-brewed?"

"I will taste the home-brewed," replied Lancelot, "and will, with your permission, go inside, as I wish to consult you on a very interesting subject."

Tom Tidy's face darkened a little, for he suspected that the "interesting subject" could be no other than Patty; but the frown subsided as he arose and led the way into the room that served him for parlour, drawing-room, and library. Mrs. Tidy followed with the jug of home-brewed.

Lancelot wished the business over and went straight to the point.

"Mr. Tidy, I won't waste words in what I

am going to say. I love Patty, truly and honourably, and I have come to ask your consent to our marriage."

"Mr. Wyld," said the blacksmith, "I like frankness, and I will be frank with you. I don't like the connection. It would be unpleasant for me, in this village, to be father-in-law to a son of the Reverend Sir Lancelot Wyld."

"But," replied Lancelot, "don't you think— begging pardon—that it will be very unpleasant to me to be denied the woman I love because you don't like my father? And won't it be very unpleasant to Patty, who loves me, and has promised to marry me sometime or other, to be refused your consent?"

"I won't consent," said Tidy, emphatically, "and there's an end of the matter!"

Lancelot put his hand in his pocket, drew out his purse, slowly opened it, and still more slowly took out a piece of paper, which he unfolded with much solemnity and deliberation.

"Read that, Mr. Tidy, and forgive Patty; and I also hope you'll forgive me."

It was a copy of the marriage certificate. Lancelot, fully aware of the probable consequences of the disclosure, resigned himself to an outburst of passion on the part of the offended father. But he was greatly surprised to notice that Tidy folded the document up again and gave it back to him with the utmost calmness.

"Young man," he said, "you have taken advantage of me. But I am one of those persons who never quarrel with the past, and who never grieve over what can't be mended. Where is Patty?" he added, turning to his wife, who left the room to prepare her for an interview with her father, which threatened to be stormy.

"There is one thing that comforts me in the matter," he continued. "You are going to take her to America, so that, if I remain in Braxford—which perhaps I shan't do—there will be no necessity why the Reverend Sir Lancelot Wyld, Baronet, and Tom Tidy, the

17 *

blacksmith, should be anything but strangers to
each other.   I shall not be obliged to have
friendly relations with him, merely because his
son married my daughter without my consent.
Does your father know of this?"

"I have told you first, for the love I bear to
Patty, and to screen her, if I can, from your
displeasure.   I have not informed my mother
even, much less my father."

" Then I advise you to do so immediately;
and from what I know of your mother I don't
think her anger will last very long. Perhaps
the case will be different with Sir Lancelot."

Lancelot was of Tidy's opinion, and had little
doubt of his mother's forgiveness. He would
have had none, if he had been quite sure that
Sir Lancelot would, as he phrased it in his own
mind, " cut up roughly," in which case his mother
would have been quite sure to take his part.

Meanwhile, his thoughts were not so much at
the Rectory as on the fast-approaching appearance of Patty in her new character. Mrs. Tidy,

who did not share her husband's dislike to Sir
Lancelot, was pleased at the turn which events
had taken, and looked with complacency on the
certainty that, if life were spared to the young
couple, her own Patty would one day be Lady
Lancelot Wyld. So she led her trembling
daughter into her father's presence, consoling
her as she went along with the assurance that,
whatever her father might say, it would be all
right in a day or two, and that she did not think
he was half so angry as he " let on " to be.

"And so," said her father, taking hold of her
hand, "you undutiful little minx! you have
jumped into the deep sea of marriage, and never
told your father what you were about. And I
have loved you since you were a baby, and
brought you up, and taken care of you, and
prized you as if you were the very apple of my
eye, and now you prove to me that you love
another man better than you love me."

" Ah, but," said Patty, her cheeks all wet
with honest tears, " but the love is so different!

There is room in my heart for both loves. One love does not drive another out, and I shall always love you as the very best of fathers; and I feel that you will forgive me, and I feel too, that if you had known Lancelot as well as I do, you would have given your consent as freely before marriage as I hope you will give it after. Won't you now?"

And she released her hand from his, without thinking what she was doing, and clasped him round the neck and kissed him.

Lancelot thought that Patty never looked so beautiful as she did at that moment, and grudged her father the kiss she bestowed upon him. But he felt very happy, and if it had not been for the knowledge that he had an ordeal yet to go through in his own family, he felt he would be the happiest fellow alive—and perhaps he was, all the same, notwithstanding.

Tidy, holding his daughter by both hands at arms length, and looking at her with feigned anger, said,

"And so, you little rebellious gipsy, you thought to get rid of your poor old father, and leave his house dark without you, did you? But perhaps you won't succeed. And perhaps your poor old father will not consent to be got rid of, and will go to America too!"

"That would be jolly," said Lancelot.

"Oh, it would be delightful," said Patty.

"And if it were not for crossing the nasty sea," said Mrs. Tidy, "I should like it too—especially as Joe is going. And I don't see why we should all be separated, and Tom and me left all alone by ourselves."

"Oh, the sea's nothing," said Tom. "Before I knew what Patty had done, and that she had a husband whom it was her duty to follow, I thought of going to America myself, to a land where there are no lords, and baronets, and dukes, and such make-believe superiors to men who are as good as they are; where land is cheap, and there is no State Church, and where Jack is as good as his master."

Lancelot had done well with Tidy, and far better than he had expected. His next task, which he would have avoided if he could have done so without paining his mother, was one which his experience in the case of Tidy told him would be better served by boldness and plain speaking than by timidity and circumlocution.

He was always afraid of his father, but he loved his mother—perhaps not so much as she loved him, but still he loved her, and could trust her. So on the following day, finding her alone, he unburthened his mind of the whole story to her, and tried hard to impress upon her the fact that, had it not been for the wholesome influence exercised over him by Patty Tidy, he might still have been leading an idle and purposeless life, without any other hope in the world than that of winning "a pot of money" on the Derby.

Lady Wyld, as has already been seen, had a favourable opinion of Patty, and had even gone so far as to fight a battle of words with her

doughty husband in favour of Patty's father,
that arch-heretic who presumed to think for
himself on a variety of theological and other
matters on which Sir Lancelot held the slightest
doubt to be iniquity. But Lady Wyld, with all
her prepossession in favour of Patty, was disappointed with her son's marriage, and more
than half inclined to be angry, especially when
she thought that he might have done openly
what he had done secretly. And she told
him so.

"Well, my dear mamma," he replied, "if I had
thought I could have been married by consent, I
would have asked for consent. But I knew it
would be of no use to ask, on account of my
father's dislike to Mr. Tidy. I knew that in
America, where I am to work and I hope to
prosper, a wife was necessary not only to my
happiness, but to my steadiness and industry;
for what's the good of working if you have nobody to work for? And I knew too, that if I
did not marry Patty, I should not marry at all;

but I hoped that, being married, neither you nor my father would continue to object to what I had done. I was prepared for anger, dearest mother, but I was also prepared when the anger had passed over, for a little forgiveness on the part of my father, and for much forgiveness from you. And Patty's a good girl, and you will not deny that she is beautiful."

"Well, she is certainly good-looking," replied Lady Wyld, "and what is more she looks good. But oh, Lancelot, how could you go and get married at a Registry Office! It's that which will vex your father more than anything. How *could* you do it?"

"It had to be done secretly, and without the fuss of banns, and all that sort of thing," replied Lancelot. "But I've got a thought, by Jove!"

His mother frowned.

"Why 'by Jove'?"

"I beg pardon. I'll never use the words again, if I can help it; but I've a thought! Really a thought!"

" Surprising ! " said his mother.

" And if it will please my father, I am sure it will please me, and I am sure it will please Patty, and I hope it will please you, whose displeasure is hard to bear.   We will be married again, in Church, in the face of all the world; and if my father will perform the ceremony, I will be the happiest fellow alive ! "   He was going to say "by Jove ! " but he refrained, and added, " the very happiest fellow in all the wide world —see if I wouldn't.   You know, I remember the sermon that my father preached last Sunday, on the text, ' There is more joy in heaven over one sinner that repenteth,' et cætera— you know the rest.   *I* will make joy in heaven, I will repent of the Registry Office, and will atone for my transgression by asking for all the rites of the Church ! "

" You absurd boy," said his mother, endeavouring to smother a laugh that twinkled in her eye in spite of her.   But she thought over the idea, and approved of it, though she was not quite sure of her husband's humour. She resolved, however, that immediately after informing Sir Lancelot of what had occurred, she would propose that a second marriage should be celebrated in Church—not at Braxford, but by special license in London.

Lady Wyld asked her son to leave the certificate with her, and as soon as her husband returned from visiting a sick old labourer in the parish, who lay at the point of death, at the age of nearly four score, she proceeded to the study to put the whole matter before him.

Sir Lancelot was startled at the intelligence, but with a woeful want of diplomacy he enlisted his wife more strongly than ever on his son's side, by an outburst of unreasonable temper.

"It's all your fault, Lady Wyld. You have spoiled the boy by your stupid indulgence, and you see what has come of it! You have let him have his own way in everything, and now, like a fool, he has gone and married beneath him. I wish you joy of the result!"

Lady Wyld was nettled at the word " stupid,"
and grew positively angry as her husband continued, " You should have left him to me, madam,"
—he always called her " madam " when he was
more than usually out of temper—" and he might
have been made a man of.   Your indulgence has
turned him into a defaulting horse-jockey, a breaker
of the fifth commandment, and a contemner of
the Church of which his father is a minister."

This was too much for Lady Wyld.

" You are not Christian-like, Sir Lancelot.
You are deficient in charity.   My boy is not a
horse-jockey, and you know it.   He has not
broken the fifth commandment.   He honours
you as far as you will let him, and he honours
and loves me.   And he does not despise or
contemn the Church of which his father is a
minister.   He asks your forgiveness for what he
has done for his own happiness—and is he not
the best judge of it?   And he wishes to be re-
married with all the rites of the Church, which,
however, I don't consider necessary."

This was a masterly thrust, though quite accidental, and carried the war into the enemy's quarters.

"Not necessary! Lady Wyld, I grieve to hear you say so. It is most absolutely necessary, and shall and must be done, and the sooner the better!"

"Then I have no more to say, Sir Lancelot," remarked the lady with a pleasant smile, and left the room without running the risk of diminishing the full result of her victory by adding another word.

Sir Lancelot saw the trap into which he had fallen, and rising from the desk where he had commenced to write his next Sunday's discourse (for he scorned to purchase lithographed sermons, and to pass them off as his own), and began to pace rapidly up and down the room.

"I shouldn't have minded so much," he thought, "if it were not for the man Tidy. How he will triumph over me! If he would but leave the village I might resign myself,

especially as the foolish boy will take his wife
away with him, and Braxford would be rid of
the whole family. But is this quite Christian
on my part? I am afraid it isn't. I am sorely
tried. And all this comes from marrying for
money. If Lady Wyld had not had a fortune in
her own right, and I had had nothing, I might
have held her in better subjection—deprived her,
to some extent, of her own way, and prevented her
from spoiling our son by her indulgence. But it
can't be helped now. The boy will do well in
America I am willing to hope and believe. But
a Registry Office marriage—in my family! It
is dreadful, awful, horrible to think of! "

Sir Lancelot again sat down to finish his
sermon. But he could not collect his thoughts,
and after two or three fitful and fruitless efforts,
he finally relinquished the effort, and sought
Lady Wyld in the drawing-room. She was
amusing herself at the pianoforte by playing
Mendelssohn's magnificent " Wedding March,"
that noble hymn of triumphant tenderness. The

last shadow of displeasure had passed from her
comely face, for it was one of her characteristics
that she never nursed anger, never sulked
or pouted, or, if it entered her mind, never
suffered an ill feeling to grow and take root
there.

Sir Lancelot's self-communion during a full
hour had tranquillised him, more or less, and
with something of fatalism—though he would
not confess to his most secret soul the existence
of such a feeling—he fell back upon the old
and consolatory philosophy of the " spilled milk "
and of " Humpty Dumpty, who could not be
set up again."

He sat down by the side of his wife, wonder-
ing a little whether she played the " Wedding
March " by design or by accident, and when she
had concluded said,

" Virginia, I don't think we should make
ourselves unhappy about Lancie's marriage,
whatever we may think of it."

" Nor I either, Lancelot. Young men and young

women will marry, whether old men and old women like it or not; and as their first object is to please themselves, and not others, I don't see—however much their elders may object beforehand—that it is of the slightest use objecting afterwards. And as the girl is a good girl, and as much a child of Eve as you and I are, and so our equal, we may just as well be pleasant as not."

"I think I could be pleasant enough," replied Sir Lancelot, "if it were not for Tidy. You must confess that with my views he is a bitter pill to swallow?"

"You must swallow him, however, to the extent at least of recognising him as your son's father-in-law. I don't mind it a bit."

"Ah, but you are not a clergyman, and you are not outraged by his disbelief."

"Thank Heaven, no!" said the lady. "Nobody's disbelief outrages me. No one can help his belief or his unbelief; and I believe Tidy to be an honest man. You are not obliged to associate with him, if you don't like."

"I should like to convert him to the true faith."

"Don't try," replied Lady Wyld. "Take your own way; let him take his."

"I shall take mine; but I do hope, for the peace of Braxford, that he'll emigrate. Meanwhile, as Lancelot's marriage is not to be undone, I think it proper that it should be made religiously as well as legally valid by the Christian rites of the Church of England, and I hope that Tidy won't raise any difficulties."

"Not he! He's too sensible a man. If it were to undo the marriage, he might, but to confirm it—oh no! Only perhaps he will not be present at the ceremony."

"I suppose not; he is too obstinate in the wrong," said Sir Lancelot with a sigh. "Yet it would be satisfactory to see him at Church on the occasion. Not that I wish it for my sake, because to me it can make no difference, but for his own."

"I guess," replied Lady Wyld, "that he won't trouble you or himself about it, and that he will stay quietly away."

But when the great day did come, and Lancelot and Patty were married by special license of the Archbishop of Canterbury, Tom Tidy and Mrs. Tidy surprised Sir Lancelot if not Lady Wyld by putting in an appearance at the ceremony.

Sir Lancelot, in order to be magnanimously Christian, extended his hand to the blacksmith, Tom Tidy shook it, not with any extraordinary warmth, however; but when a similar courtesy was offered by Lady Wyld, after she had kissed the bride, he put his whole heart into his hand, as it were, and said,

"I believe the young people will be happy, Lady Wyld, and I know they have your good wishes!"

Sir Lancelot asked the blacksmith and his wife to the wedding breakfast, but he did not do it very cordially.

18 *

"I thank you," said Tidy, "but we have
made other arrangements, which I cannot break.
But you must do me the justice, Sir Lancelot,
to allow that my family did not seek to force
itself into yours. I opposed the love of the young
people from the first; and if I am reconciled to
the marriage, it is because what has been has
been, and because what is *is*, and neither you
nor I can make it otherwise."

And the blacksmith took his departure, with
a kindly glance at Lady Wyld, and escorted his
wife to dinner at the Crystal Palace.

Before Lancelot and his bride took their departure for Virginia, they were invited to a family
party at Mill Haughton.   The bride, without
knowing, though not without suspecting, had to
pass through the ordeal of friendly or unfriendly
criticism on the part of all the ladies, and on
that of some of the gentlemen present.

Mrs. Haughton thought her a "sonsie and a
bonnie lassie." Miss Esther thought she was
rather "dowdy." Miss Euphemia thought she

was genuine and true-hearted, and that she had
in her, in the rough, all the elements that combine to form the true woman as well as the true
lady.   The bridegroom's mother thought she
wanted nothing but a little more social intercourse with the world to become a charming
woman.   Herbert Haughton thought she would
make a first-rate model of Phyllis, though her
husband did not exactly suit his taste for a
Corydon.

Colonel Haughton thought what a young fool
his nephew was to sell the freedom of his whole
life for a pretty face, that in a few years would
be pretty no longer, and congratulated himself
that in his youth and early manhood he had
successfully resisted all such temptation; while
Mr. Haughton himself was strongly of opinion
that Lancelot had done the right thing, and that
marriage would be the salvation of him.

In less than a month after these events,
Matilda Jennings finally refused the hand of Joe
Tidy, and accepted that of Harry Talmadge, the

organist. Joe did not grieve overmuch, but accompanied Lancelot and his bride to Virginia with a light heart and a determination to make his fortune.

Tom Tidy, to the great satisfaction of Sir Lancelot, only remained in Braxford for about three months, sold the good-will of his business, turned all his effects into ready money, and set sail for the New World with the kindly good wishes of all the people of the village.

The Rev. Sir Lancelot regretted his departure—at least, he said so; but Lady Wyld had her doubts whether the regret were not simulated, though she took care never to breathe a word on the subject to her husband, or to anyone else.

CHAPTER XV.

It was expected that Oscar Lebrun would have attended the family gathering at Mill Haughton to meet Lancelot Wyld and his bride, and to wish them God speed in their voyage to Virginia. But Oscar was detained in London on business of urgent importance, and wrote that he would pay his respects to the couple at Baggs's, where they were to remain for a few days before proceeding to Liverpool.

He also wrote to his betrothed that he would leave London for Swinston on a day not very distant, which he fixed. This information was conveyed in the short postscript of a long and fervent letter, such as lovers who are really in love take pleasure in writing, and such as lovers who really and truly reciprocate the love expressed for them take delight in reading. And Euphemia patiently awaited his coming, feeding her mind with pleasant thoughts, in a solitude of which she never wearied so long as it was filled with remembrances of him.

The promised day came—but not Oscar. Neither did he send a letter to explain his absence. Another day passed, and surprise and alarm began to be felt in the Haughton household. The surprise was general; the alarm was confined to the gentle bosom of Euphemia.

When a week had elapsed and no answer had been returned to letters of inquiry, the anxiety of Euphemia became distressing to all around her. To relieve her over-wrought feelings she wrote to her brother Herbert, requesting him to call at Oscar's lodgings in Lisle Street, Soho, to make personal inquiry. She feared that so devoted a lover must be ill and unable to write, or that some unknown calamity had befallen him.

Herbert had taken a liking to Oscar, though at first disposed to regard him with jealous hostility, or at least with coldness, and readily undertook the mission.

Though a Londoner by long residence, he was not well acquainted with the purlieus of Soho and Leicester Squares, where French artificers and political refugees love to congregate, and where they form a shabby little Paris in the heart of an alien city.

He wandered through the narrow streets, once the centre of fashionable London, and looked at the exterior of the dingy hotels and restaurants, the forlorn *cafés* and *charcuteries*, where, notwithstanding the absence of outside show, very good *comestibles* were to be obtained at moderate prices, and at the wine shops, where varieties of good Bordeaux and Burgundy, red and white, of which the very names were unknown to the Londoners, were to be had at a moderate outlay. He also looked in at the windows of the newsvendors and tobacconists, where the unwholesome comic literature of Paris was displayed in all its obscene luxuriance, and wondered whether there was an obscene public to purchase such trash in sufficient numbers to recompense its purveyors.

He at last made his way to Lisle Street, and rang the bell at the door of the house indicated. The bell was answered by an aged Frenchwoman, with a red and yellow handkerchief tied round her brow in antique fashion by way of headdress, who very speedily exhausted her modest stock of English in her replies to his questions.

Herbert informed her in French that he was a relative of M. Oscar Lebrun, and that he had been deputed by other relatives at a distance, who had expected him on a visit, and who had neither seen nor heard from him, to make inquiries, lest he should be ill, or lest any misfortune should have befallen him. The landlady looked very grave.

"Monsieur Oscar has not been here for six days. He promised to return on the evening of the day he left. We have heard nothing of him. We know nothing of him. Would monsieur like to see my husband, Monsieur Grenier?"

Herbert said he would. But M. Grenier was not at home. He was a pianoforte maker, and was at work in the factory, and would not return until the evening. Would monsieur call again? Her husband's hours were uncertain. Monsieur said he would return again at eight o'clock, if that would not be too early.

It was about the time that "mon mari" would most probably be at home. Would monsieur please to leave his name? Herbert handed her his card.

Having an hour to spare preparatory to calling for Colonel Haughton at the Club at which they had agreed to dine that day with Colonel MacTavish, he took another leisurely stroll through the dismal district, and wondered why Oscar Lebrun, in his new position, with fortune at command, should have taken up his residence, even temporarily, in such a quarter, unless it were from the force of old habit and association, or perhaps a preference for the society of his quasi-countrymen.

As he walked along his attention was attracted by a *café* of superior appearance, at the door of which stood a young woman with a bundle of French newspapers, copies of which she was offering for sale.

Herbert purchased one, and entered the *café* to read it at leisure, for the French news was exciting, and the fortunes of France seemed to be at the mercy of the victorious Prussians.

He had some difficulty in obtaining a place at one of the little marble tables provided for the accommodation of the guests, for the *café* was full of men, smoking, drinking absinthe, playing at dominoes, or reading the papers, while some few were discussing the news, speaking all at once, and in a state of apparently all but frantic excitement.

At last he found a seat, called for absinthe—

not because he liked it, but because it reminded
him of Parisian life, and because he did not like
to look singular.

He speedily exhausted the meagre news in the
paper—which was but a repetition, with a Communistic gloss, of that in the London journals of
the morning—and noticed, without appearing to
do so, that one of the company, a handsome old
man, with snow-white hair and flowing white
beard, with a tinge of golden yellow at the tips,
had fixed his large grey eyes attentively upon him.

He at once recognised Rabagaud, the Communist, the orator of the Boulevards, to whose
discourse to the people, he and his uncle when
accompanied by Oscar Lebrun, had listened on
their last visit to Paris.

Rabagaud seemed to have some remembrance
of him; but Herbert, not desiring his further
acquaintance, paid for his absinthe and took his
departure.

Colonel Haughton, as his nephew well knew,
never liked to talk about business, or anything

that was in the least degree unpleasant, at the
dinner-table, and it was not until the two
Colonels and their guest had mounted to the
Club smoking-room to indulge in the eternal
cigar, the transmutation of which into smoke
and ashes seems to form half the business of
many men's lives, that Herbert informed his
companions of the mission that had been entrusted to him by his sister, and of the suspicious
circumstance of Oscar's disappearance that he had
already discovered.

" It looks ugly," said Colonel Haughton.

" Infernally ugly ! " added Colonel MacTavish;
" and I shouldn't wonder if the young man had
been robbed and murdered."

" But by whom? " inquired Herbert.

" Why," answered Colonel Haughton, promptly,
" by some of the rascally French Communists and
conspirators with whom he is suspected to have
had dealings already, and with the leaders of
whom he is known to have been in some mysterious manner connected."

" Shouldn't wonder at all," added the other Colonel. " I should follow up this clue, if it be a clue, were it the case of anyone in whom I was interested. Your new cousin, as I understand, is a regular and proper young man, and not likely to have absconded for debt or any other reason ? "

" Not at all likely," replied Herbert. " He lived upon half of his earnings when a workman, is heir to a title and a hundred thousand pounds, and engaged to be married to one of the loveliest girls in England. Why should he abscond ? "

" I did not even suspect, though I mentioned it," said MacTavish. " But don't you think there must have been foul play somewhere? "

" He didn't drink, did he? " inquired Colonel Haughton. " He didn't look like it, anyhow."

" He was sober, not to say abstemious," replied Herbert. " He drank nothing stronger than *vin ordinaire*, and he always mixed it with water."

" It is very remarkable. Has he suffered from sunstroke, do you think, and become unconscious?

Did he carry any papers or cards in his pocket that would show who he was in case of accident ?"

" I can't tell," replied Herbert; " I don't know ; but I'm going at eight o'clock to Lisle Street, to ascertain what I can from the landlord of his lodgings, a Frenchman. Will either of you go with me ?"

" Better go alone," said MacTavish. " If the French Working Men's League has anything to do with Mr. Lebrun's disappearance, and his landlord is a member of the gang, it would frighten him if we both, or either of us, went along with you to be witnesses of your conversation. It would put him on his guard ; and it would be better for you to be on your guard yourself, young man. Get all you can out of him, without seeming to try to get anything out of him—that is to say, pump him without creaking the pump-handle. We'll wait here until you return, and you can bring us news of your clue, and whether you think it is a clue worth following up.   You will find us in the billiard-room."

Herbert proceeded alone to Lisle Street, and found M. Grenier in his shirt-sleeves, smoking, with a glass of absinthe before him, and thought as he looked at him that he recognised him as having been at the *café* that afternoon, sitting at the same table with M. Rabagaud.

M. Grenier was a stout, under-sized man of about fifty, with a large round head covered with black hair, cut short like stubble, with a black moustache, which would have been accompanied by whiskers and beard of the same colour and texture had Nature been allowed to have her way, but which were all close-shaven, leaving on the face and chin a large superficies of purply black, that showed the growing roots of the hair, in despite of the razor.

He was not an attractive-looking person, and his strongly-built frame, brawny arms, and great rough hands, showed the athlete, trained or un-trained, whom it would not be pleasant or safe for anyone not an athlete by nature or by culture to have encountered in enmity.

Herbert did not feel quite comfortable at being alone with him, and would have been glad of the presence of either of the Colonels whom he had left at the Club. But he thought, having been invited to take a seat, that it was best to proceed to business.

"You have my card, Monsieur Grenier," he said in French, "and know both my name and my business, I presume?"

"Perfectly well," replied M. Grenier. "You come to make inquiries about this good Monsieur Oscar Lebrun, who has left his apartments suddenly, and without taking anyone into his confidence. But that is not a very extraordinary thing in a young man, is it? *Que voulez-vous?*"

"I think it very extraordinary in this particular young man," replied Herbert, "who, for personal and family reasons of great importance, promised to be at Swinston in the Fens several

days ago, and who has neither appeared there
nor written to explain his absence."

"*Mais, que voulez-vous?*" said M. Grenier,
looking at the smoke of his cigar as it curled
upwards. "I know nothing of his movements.
He is not accountable to me for what he does,
neither am I accountable to anybody else for his
regularity or irregularity. *Ma foi!* he is not a
son of mine, and he goes and comes as he
pleases, without giving me any right, even if I
had the inclination, to question him. *Que voulez-
vous?*"

"Pardon me if I ask," replied Herbert, "did
he leave his table or papers in confusion, as if he
meant to return, or did he pack up his effects as
if he had pre-arranged his departure?"

"I think," said M. Grenier, after a long pause,
and two or three deliberate whiffs at the cigar,
and as many deliberate surveys of the curls of
the smoke as he blew it out of his mouth, "that
he left his writing-table in its ordinary confusion,
with papers and letters lying about, and that

19 *

nothing has been removed since he left. *Que voulez-vous?*"

"Could I be allowed to look at his writing-table and the papers he left on it?" asked Herbert. "Perhaps some memorandum for my family, which might explain his movements, might be found among them."

The question seemed to puzzle M. Grenier considerably, and it was a considerable time—or at least it appeared so to Herbert—before he replied, smoking vigorously all the while.

"I don't know," he said at last. "I will consult Madame Grenier." And so saying he went to the door, calling lustily, "Suzanne! Suzanne!"

Suzanne, in the person of Madame Grenier, with her red and yellow handkerchief around her head, answered the summons, and was asked if she saw any objection to showing Monsieur the room of M. Lebrun, and whether it were still in the state in which he left it.

"Not exactly," said Madame Grenier; "Monsieur Lebrun was untidy with his papers, and in dusting them I had to arrange them. But all is there that he left. But Monsieur is not a Commissaire de Police, is he? And has he any authority to examine things?" And then she added, *sotto voce*, to her husband, " Be careful, *mon ami*, be careful!"

Monsieur Grenier took the hint.

" Monsieur will excuse us; we are poor people in a strange country, and we live, *ma foi!* in evil times, and we think, both of us, that we cannot allow anyone to look over the papers of Monsieur Lebrun without authority. Perhaps, who knows? Monsieur Lebrun may return to-night, or to-morrow, at any moment, and what should we say to him if we allowed anyone in his absence to look into his secrets? For there may be secrets, you know, and they are quite secret for my wife and me; for she cannot read English, and I am not an *espion*, or a *mouchard*, but a man of honour, *corbleu!*"

Herbert saw there was no use in pressing the

point, and prepared to bring the interview to a close, merely saying as he rose to depart,

" There would be no danger with me, Monsieur Grenier. Monsieur Oscar Lebrun is my cousin, the head of our family, and betrothed to my sister. It is not strange that we should be anxious about him, indeed it would be strange if we were not."

" That goes without saying," replied M. Grenier. " I wish I could give you any information ; but perhaps there will be no cause for inquietude ; he may reappear. He is not obliged to tell everybody his business, and why he leaves home. I have your address" (pulling Herbert's card from a leather purse), "and if I hear any news of him, I will inform you; yes, immediately."

M. Grenier accompanied his visitor to the door, and bade him good-night with what the French call effusion, and Herbert returned to his uncle and Colonel MacTavish at the Club. He found them both in their shirt-sleeves in the billiard-room.

He sat down and watched the players until the game was concluded, when the two Colonels, one on each side of him, came to learn the result of his interview with the Frenchman. It was soon told, and was as unsatisfactory to the listeners as it had been to the reciter.

"Be hanged if I don't think," said Mac-Tavish, "that the fellow knows a great deal more than he likes to tell. That's why he keeps a quiet tongue in his head. These French Communists are a dangerous lot."

"But we don't know that he is a Communist," said Herbert.

"We don't know," said Colonel Haughton, "but we may suspect. Half the French in London are Communists or political refugees, or conspirators of some kind; and I think, if nothing is heard of Oscar Lebrun—or, I beg pardon, Haughton—during the next three days, that we should set the detectives on Monsieur Grenier."

"What detectives?" asked MacTavish some-

what tartly. " Not the private detectives surely?
A set of fellows who, in my opinion, are meaner,
more cowardly, and more rascally than any
rascals they pretend to ferret out." It was one
of MacTavish's hobbies to abuse the professional
spy system. " Scoundrels! " he said; " I would
make their dirty trade a felony, and allow no
detective officers, except among the police, responsible to their superiors and the Government,
and having no private interest to serve."

" Well," said Colonel Haughton, anxious to
avoid a discussion on a subject which he knew,
from old experience, was likely, if in the least
degree encouraged, to become both angry and
prolonged, " I mean the police, of course. The
interest of the private detective is to make
money, that of the police to discover the truth.
We are agreed upon the point, and there is no
more to be said."

" I think," remarked Herbert, " that we
should allow a day or two to elapse before proceeding further. Oscar may return in the

meantime, and there may be no necessity for further action."

Colonel Haughton agreed; and it was decided that three days, and no more, should be allowed for the taking of ulterior measures to discover what had become of Oscar Lebrun, and Herbert retired to think how best he should communicate the news to his sister.

CHAPTER XVI.

THE news was altogether distressing to the good people at Mill Haughton. Miss Esther, somewhat soured by her recent little experience of mankind, was of opinion—though she took care not to say so—that Oscar Lebrun, if all the truth were known, was not much better than Lord O'Monaghan. Mrs. Haughton thought the poor lad had been taken ill in the streets, or far away from his home on a journey, perhaps, without any kind women folk to look after him. Mr. Haughton, who knew how exemplary Oscar's behaviour had always been, thought that nothing worse had happened than the miscarriage of a letter announcing his departure to France to see his relatives, whom it was known he desired to visit; while poor Euphemia, who knew a little, though not all, concerning his former relations with the secret societies of Paris, which had ramifications all over Great Britain and the Continent, was more apprehensive than she cared to tell of trouble and treachery.

Her brother's letter was not calculated to remove her fears, and his account of M. Grenier was not consolatory, inasmuch as his reticence seemed to hint of a mystery, which he could elucidate if disposed.

Day after day passed wearily away, to Euphemia, amid her constantly-increasing anxiety, and still the Post Office brought her nothing but vague messages from her brother that no further information had been obtained.

Colonel Haughton, being an idle man, who had nothing to do but read the newspapers at the Club, order his dinner, and talk with his brother members about politics, the play, the

weather, or the latest town scandal, happened to
mention Oscar's disappearance, over his chop
and pint of claret, to a crony as idle as himself.
Crony the first mentioned it to crony the second,
and crony the second to crony the third, and so
on, until the story, spreading like ripples in a
pond, to an ever-increasing circle, reached the
all-receptive ears of the London correspondent of
a country journal, by whom it was forthwith put
into print.

Small and personal London news is generally
unknown to the great body of the London public
until it comes back from the outer circumference
of the provinces to the centres of intelligence
whence it sprang; and it was in this manner and
at second-hand that the London daily journals
announced a " Mysterious Disappearance," which
in ambiguous phraseology was described as that of
a young, handsome, and unmarried nobleman, who
had recently succeeded to a title and a fortune
under romantic circumstances.

The paragraph in due course found its way

into the columns of the "Swinston Dove" of the Wednesday and the "Swinston Scorpion" of the Saturday, and set the tongues of all the male and female gossips, and of the Fen country generally, wagging more energetically than they had wagged before on the subject of Oscar Lebrun.

Of course everybody in the neighbourhood knew to whom the statement referred, though the Londoners, when the paragraph appeared, and long afterwards, were densely ignorant of the missing man's name and title.

Mr. Octavius Little, aware of the case, inasmuch as he had been consulted upon it, called upon Mr. Haughton to advise ulterior measures, by the detective police or otherwise, to throw light upon the mystery, but was stopped in his advice by Mr. Haughton, who handed him a letter which he had that morning received, and the contents of which he had not yet disclosed to his daughter Euphemia or any member of the family.

It made no illusion to the " Mysterious Disappearance of a Nobleman," was signed by
the Physician of one of the London hospitals,
and stated that a patient—who had been ten
days in the establishment, who had no cards or
documents on his person to afford any clue to
his identity, and who had been delirious until
the morning or the afternoon of which the letter
was written—had represented that Mr. Haughton,
M.P., of Mill Haughton, was his nearest relative
in England.   He was too ill to be removed, and
the Doctor strongly urged that Mr. Haughton, or
someone on his behalf, should visit the sick man
immediately.

" Do you think that this is the missing Lord
Ravelstone?" asked the lawyer.

" I think it highly probable, and have resolved,
at all events, to go and see.   I shall start this
evening.   I would ask you to come with me, as
legal advice may be necessary, only the notice
may be too short for a man of your years."

"Bother my years!" said Mr. Little.   " I

am only sixty, and you, I take it, are near upon fifty-seven. What *you* can do *I* can do. I shall be ready."

"Excuse my exaggeration of your venerability. Every man thinks his contemporaries, even if they are of the same year, much older than himself. He sees the changes in them, but he does not see the changes in himself, even if he looks in the glass, for he thinks the glass lies, and if he feels young, he imagines that he *is* young."

"So he is, if he truly thinks so," replied the lawyer. "We will leave together at eight, reach London by midnight, and see the mysterious patient in the morning. I shall telegraph to the Doctor to say so."

Mr. Haughton informed the ladies of the letter —for Euphemia looked so pale and woe-begone, and drooped so visibly from day to day that he was glad to infuse a little hope into her mind, even if the hope should turn out to be fallacious. Better a gleam of false hope, he thought, than a settled melancholy, unbroken by a gleam.

"And if it *is* Oscar," said Euphemia, "you must telegraph immediately, and I will come up."

"Not alone, my dearie," replied her mother. "You and I will go thegither."

"Yes, I would advise it," said Mr. Haughton; "but 'hooly and fairly,' as you say in Scotland. We must first be sure, and then we can make all requisite arrangements. If this be Oscar Lebrun, there is evidently a change for the better in his condition, whatever that condition may be, and whatever may have been the circumstances that produced it. And I will not fail to telegraph as soon as I am sure of what I have to communicate."

Mr. Haughton and Mr. Little, accompanied by Herbert Haughton, presented themselves at the hospital, and were informed by the resident medical gentleman in attendance that the patient had been found insensible on the pavement at midnight in Gerrard Street, Soho, eleven days previously. The police discovered blood on the pavement, and on examination found that he was wounded. They had him removed without delay to the hospital, where it was found that he was suffering from a gun-shot wound in the breast, at the base of the right shoulder. He was treated with all the care and attention required.

The police notified the facts in the usual way, with a view of discovering the identity of the wounded man. Several people had called to see him, but all failed to recognise him, and no information could be obtained from himself, as his mind wandered and he spoke incoherently, the only recognisable word he uttered being " Euphemia."

On the previous day, after a long and refreshing sleep, he awoke to a greater degree of consciousness than he had previously exhibited, and expressed a wish that Mr. Haughton of Mill Haughton should be informed of his condition and requested to come and see him.

The word " Euphemia " was sufficient to Mr.

Haughton and his son to point to the identity
of the wounded man, and almost sufficient for
the cautious legal mind of Mr. Octavius Little.

The patient still slept when the three gentlemen arrived, a circumstance that did not prevent
the Physician from leading them to the bed-side.
It was indeed Oscar Lebrun, but pale and
emaciated.

"I think he will do well now," said the nurse,
in a whisper, an opinion in which the Doctor
coincided.

"No vital part has been injured; but there
has been considerable fever, and the delirium
was alarming at first. It is possible it proceeded
from mental causes strongly at work within a
weakened body. I think he will recover. Will
you come into my room and tell me what you
know of him?"

Mr. Haughton told the Doctor the whole story
and the relationship in which the young man
stood towards himself and his family, and expressed at the same time his wonder at the

attempt that had been made on his life, for he
did not suppose that it could have been the
result of accident or chance merely, but more
probably of private vengeance.

"We shall hear the explanation from himself
in a day or two," said the Doctor, "or at least
I hope so."

Mr. Haughton forthwith sent a telegram to
his wife, for the information of the family—but
more especially of the anxious Euphemia—that
Oscar Lebrun was discovered; that he had been
wounded, but not fatally; no one as yet knew
by whom or with what object; that he was convalescent and going on favourably.   He also
promised that further particulars would be communicated in another telegram.

The three gentlemen partook of an early dinner
at the Whiggamore Club, leaving directions at
their hostelry where they were to be seen in case
of a summons from the hospital.

They found nothing to talk about, as was
natural, but the attempted assassination of Oscar

20 *

Lebrun, and wondered greatly why such a deed could have been committed in the streets of London without exciting a commotion in the Press and in the public mind, whereas, as far as they knew, it had passed *sub silentio*, and excited no remark, except, perhaps, in the hospital.

"Had he been killed outright," said Mr. Little, "there would have been a Coroner's inquest, and all the rest of it; but an abortive attempt, you see, only receives abortive notice. Perhaps, had he died in the hospital, little or nothing would have been heard of it. We live so fast now-a-days that we don't remember anything above four and twenty hours, unless there be some great scandal to be gloated over or some great mystery to be unravelled. Then we attach ourselves to it, partly for the love of the scandal, and in as great a degree for the love of the mystery."

"But there is a mystery about this case," replied Herbert, "and a very ugly mystery too, and I trust we shall, as you say, unravel it. I

suspect the hand of the secret societies of the
Continent in it. I know he has had relations
with them."

"One would think," said Mr. Haughton,
"that they had enough to do at home just now.
The mischief go with them! They have their
ramifications all over Europe. They are not
only the enemies of men of their own class, who
dare to have wills of their own, and energies and
abilities superior to the common ruck of the lazy
and ignorant multitude, but the enemies of the
industry they pretend to regulate."

"I have never studied the matter," replied
the lawyer. "From the little I know of them
they appear to me to be wild and crack-brained
enthusiasts, with good intentions."

"Hang their good intentions!" said the elder
Mr. Haughton. "I hate the phrase! In the
mind of a stupid person a good intention may be
as mischievous as a match struck by a fool to
give light in a powder magazine. Good intentions! The Jews who crucified the Saviour had

good intentions. Good intentions are no excuse for anything. I prefer bad intentions, for I can be on my guard against them. But as for good intentions, no one is safe from them."

"Don't excite yourself," said the lawyer. "Everything that's good *is* good, according to its degree, and good intentions among the rest."

"I won't admit it," replied Mr. Haughton. "The vivisectionists have good intentions. The burglar has good intentions—towards himself. Torquemada was a man of the most excellent intentions. Calvin burned Servetus with good intentions. And who had better intentions than Robespierre and Marat? Perhaps the Devil, when he was leader of a rebellion in Heaven, and became, as Sydney Smith said, the first Reformer, had, according to his lights, the very best of intentions. A good intention is no excuse for obstinacy, it is no excuse for stupidity, least of all is it an excuse for misguided philanthropy. I do believe that there is sometimes more malignity in the heart of a professional

philanthropist—such as Robespierre, for instance
—than in that of a professional house-breaker."

"It amuses you to be extravagant," said the
lawyer, "and to be paradoxical. You take a
dram of strong language as other people take a
stimulant, and it does you good, I suppose."

"Well, I think it does," replied Mr. Haughton.
"It lets off steam. It acts as a relief to the
overcharged feelings."

There came no summons from the hospital
that evening, but early on the following morning
a note from the Doctor invited Mr. Haughton
to visit his patient alone and unattended. He
thought the excitement of many visitors might
perhaps be too much for Oscar's slowly returning
strength, or if not, that it would be injudicious
to burden it by over-excitement.

Mr. Haughton obeyed the call, and found Oscar
calm and collected, but weak, and highly gratified
to see him. His first inquiry was for Euphemia,
and how had she borne his apparent breach of
faith in not coming to Swinston as promised.

" She always believed that a satisfactory explanation would be forthcoming, but she never dreamed, I think, of such an explanation as this."

" I knew she would trust me," said Oscar faintly, " that is, as soon as I was able to think; for the last few days have been a blank to me—not exactly a blank, perhaps, because my mind, or what remained of it, was a chaos of unhappy and contradictory dreams, and terrors, and absurdities, amid which Euphemia's face shone like a star. But I am better now. I think the danger has passed."

" Keep calm," said Mr. Haughton ; " don't excite yourself. You can tell me some other time what happened to you."

" I can tell you now," replied Oscar. And he narrated the story in few, but clear words. He had been summoned to attend a special meeting of a branch lodge of the " Maireann," sitting in London—he declined to say where—and had been requested to define his future relationship to the body, and to contribute a very large portion of the money the members had been informed he was to inherit to the future support of the Society, and to the dissemination of its principles in Russia, Germany, France, Belgium, Great Britain, and the United States.

He had then formally renounced his membership, on the ground that the leaders advocated doctrines that were subversive of all society, and that would be ruinous to the working classes themselves, if they could be carried into practice. Whatever means he could spare—and he was inclined to be liberal—he would cheerfully contribute to the education and the national union of the working classes for their mutual benefit and advantage; but he positively refused to lend his name or give his aid to projects for the subversion of all Governments and of all religion, and for the superseding of the established order of society and of morals. He was opposed to capital punishment, opposed to the conscription, which made soldiers of men who would rather be

labourers, and opposed to the privileges of the
few, that had to be paid for by the many; but he
would not aid in the establishment of a compul-
sory equality among men whom God and Nature
made unequal, and the levelling down of the
able and the wise to the low standard of the
incapable and the foolish. He finally stated his
intention to withdraw from the Society, and was
met with cries of,

"Impossible, impossible! Once a member
always a member; the bond is indissoluble, only
to be broken by death!"

In the midst of the confusion created by his
speech, he made his way from the room, went
quietly downstairs, and proceeded towards his
lodgings in Lisle Street. He had been—as far
as he remembered—about five minutes in the
street, when he heard footsteps behind him, and
a voice that called him by name. He turned
round, recognised two men whom he knew, and
immediately saw the flash of fire-arms, and fell
wounded on the ground. He remembered no

more until he found himself in the hospital,
and had recovered sufficient consciousness to
inform the Physician of Mr. Haughton's name,
and request his presence. This was the whole
story.

Mr. Haughton, as he listened, resolved in his
own mind that the arm of the law should be
invoked to punish this dastardly attempt at
assassination, and to show the Socialists and
Communists, and crazy fanatics of the Labour
question at home and abroad, that no immunity
of secrecy and numbers should avail to bring
the malefactors face to face with justice.

"Could you identify your assailants?" he
asked.

"Yes; I know them," replied Oscar, "but I
do not wish to identify them. I wish nothing
further to be done. What others might have
done if my life had been sacrificed, I do
not care to think of; but as I live, and value my
life for the sake of one dearer to me than myself,
I do not desire to stir in the matter."

"But for the sake of outraged humanity," urged Mr. Haughton, "for the sake of public justice, such a crime should not go unpunished, merely because it has not been fatal!"

"I beg of you," said Oscar, "for Euphemia's sake, to take no further step. I am a marked man already; but I may escape further persecution if I keep quiet. The men cannot be identified, except by me. I will not identify them, for, if they were identified and punished, my life would not be worth twenty-four hours' purchase. What is, *is*. I live, and hope to live, and I will let well alone."

The Doctor, entering, noticed that the patient was much excited, and counselled Mr. Haughton to adjourn until another day all further conversation on that or any other subject. The counsel was a command, and Mr. Haughton retired to send a consoling telegram to Swinston, and to consult with Mr. Little and his son Herbert.

"I do not speak as a lawyer," said Mr. Little, when the story was told him, "but as a friend.

As a lawyer, I would go to the very root of this matter, ferret out the guilty parties, and bring them to condign punishment.   But as a friend, I think Lord Ravelstone—Mr. Oscar, I mean— is right, and that it might endanger his peace of mind, if not his life, and certainly retard his recovery, if any publicity were given to the matter, or any step whatever were taken to bring the assassins to justice.   What has to be done is to remove the patient from the hospital at the earliest advisable moment, and take him to your own house, Mr. Haughton—I think that would be the best—and bestow upon him the care and attention he needs.   I say your own house emphatically, as soon as he is able to travel; for there is one lady there, I think, the very sight of whom will work more than half his cure, and who, if I do not judge wrongly, will be worth more to him than a whole army of Doctors."

Mr. Haughton was of the same opinion; but it was fully a week before the convalescent could be safely removed.   During that time, however, there was a change in the *personnel* of the visitors to the hospital.

Mr. Haughton and Mr. Little returned home, having accomplished their mission, and their place was more than supplied by Mrs. Haughton and Euphemia, who paid constant visits to the invalid, and had the satisfaction of seeing a daily increase of his strength.

At the end of the week he was able to return to Swinston and take up his residence with his old landlady, Mrs. Stebbings, in the High Street, refusing the offered hospitality of Mill Haughton until he could enter the shrine of his divinity as her destined lord and conqueror, and bear her off in triumph.

It is an old saying that there is "many a slip 'twixt the cup and the lip;" and the union of Oscar and Euphemia Haughton was fixed for a certain early day, when an unforeseen and painful catastrophe caused its postponement for two months.

The gay and gallant Colonel Haughton, who

lived but for himself and his dinners, who had invested all he possessed in the purchase of an annuity for his own life, so that no one, as he thought, might have an interest in his death, and so that he might derive from his money all the advantage which it was possible that money could bring ; who had systematically scorned marriage, and pitied the poor fools who linked themselves to women, was destined " to point a moral and adorn a tale," and afford a new exemplification of the old truth, that it is not good for man to be alone.

It was noticed at the three Clubs of which Colonel Haughton was a member that he had not made his appearance at either of them for four days, and his various acquaintances began to wonder whether the gallant gentleman had not been taken ill; and it struck his very particular crony, Colonel MacTavish, that it behoved him to call at the Colonel's chambers to make inquiries.

He called. The Colonel had, in the slang of

the day, " sported oak," that is, the outer door remained closed, as a certification that the in-dweller was not at home.

He summoned the housekeeper, who looked after all the chambers, who informed him that the Colonel had most probably gone out of town, on which occasions he had given orders that his rooms should not be opened or entered without his special authority. No such authority had been given in this instance.

Colonel MacTavish, promising to call again on the morrow, took his departure. On the morrow he reappeared. The " oak " was still " sported."

" Mrs. Jones," he said ; " or, I beg pardon if your name is Smith—"

" Barnett," she replied, curtseying.

" Well, Mrs. Barnett, you have the key of the Colonel's chambers. They must require airing after being shut up for five days. Please bring it, and let me enter. I am his friend, as you know, and I am anxious about him."

"I have seed you here with him," replied Mrs. Barnett, with another curtsey, "and I'll open the door, if you tell me to do so; but you must tell Colonel Haughton when he comes back that you desired me."

"All right," said MacTavish, slipping half-a-crown into her hand. "Bring me the key."

She brought it. Colonel MacTavish opened the door and entered. A ghastly spectacle presented itself. In the sitting-room, his head upon the fender, in a circle of blood that had dried upon the floor, lay the dead body of the unfortunate Colonel Haughton, stark and cold!

"Good God!" said MacTavish; "this is dreadful. How can it have happened?"

"Oh deary me!" said Mrs. Barnett. "The poor gentleman must have had a fit, and fallen on the fender and cut his head open! Oh, the poor dear, and nobody to help him! Oh, if there had been somebody in the room, it might have been different."

"Oh, yes!" said MacTavish, greatly shocked.

III.   21

" If he had had a wife, or a daughter, or any of woman kind within call. It is horrible to think of ! And he so sprightly, and did not know that he was growing old ! Did not know that he required a companion ! Hated women, poor fellow ! "

" Are you quite sure ? " inquired Mrs. Barnett. " *I* am not. I am afraid he only hated to marry them."

" Well, let that pass," said MacTavish. " It is a dreadful business. You must notify the Coroner. What a world we live in ! "

The inquest was duly held, and a verdict of accidental death returned, and there was an end of the earthly record of poor Colonel Haughton, who cared for nobody, and who cared for nothing except his dinner and his ease. It cannot be said that he died regretted ; even his nephew and Colonel MacTavish, the two people whom he cared—perhaps one fifteenth or one twentieth of one per cent.—about, had no particular sorrow to spare for him, or any particular admiration to bestow upon his memory. His fortune, such as it was, perished with him. He left no will, for he had nothing to leave, and his few little personal trinkets, of no great value, came to Mr. Haughton of Mill Haughton, as his next of kin. He lived up to his income, did not get into debt, and had just enough money left in the bank to pay for his funeral expenses and the rent of his chambers.

The marriage of Oscar Lebrun, otherwise Lord Ravelstone (he had an unconquerable aversion to assume the title), took place at Swinston two months after the death of Colonel Haughton. The bells of Swinston rang merry peals! Beer was given away in hogsheads; the paupers in the workhouse were treated to dinner, tea, and tobacco; largesses were given to all the local charities; the workmen in Mr. Haughton's mills were regaled, and spoken to and at, in speeches of all degrees of eloquence, real or mock, and there was a gala time in the little town.

The bride and bridegroom departed to the Western Highlands of Argyllshire, where they hoped to be and were alone, for a happy three months, far from care and the " Maircann," far from everything and everybody but their own happy selves.

He is often urged, especially by his father-in-law, to take his seat in the House of Lords, and give that illustrious assembly, and the country, the benefit of his great experience on the labour question, and the critical relations that are gradually growing up between the employers and the employed, in all parts of the civilised world; but though he does not absolutely refuse, he persistently procrastinates and postpones decision. But having an active mind, and not being without ambition, he thinks that the day will come when he may enter the political arena, and that when it comes, he will do his best to be of service to his country and to humanity.

Miss Esther Haughton, at the date of "last advices," as merchants and newspapers say, still

hovered between the Rev. Hope Smithers and
Mr. Barnard Strutt; but Mr. Barnard Strutt, the
rich man, was growing in favour, and Mr. Hope
Smithers, the poor man, was losing it.

Lord O'Monaghan married the very old lady
who, though she paid all his debts, took care to
have all her money settled strictly upon herself,
with an annuity to his Lordship in case he should
survive her, which bequest, however, she reserved
to herself the power to annul at any time, if his
Lordship, put on his good behaviour, did not
comport himself exactly as she wished. But in
the meanwhile she was not illiberal, and allowed
him a generous amount of pocket money.

Lady Augusta Pippins erased him from her
visiting list, and though he entertained a vague
hope of a Colonial Governorship, the hope grew
daily fainter, and bade fair to be wholly and
speedily extinguished.

Mr. Herbert Haughton devotes himself to art.
He has not forgotten the beautiful model who
escaped from his grasp, but thinks, upon the

whole, that for him, at all events, the escape was lucky. He has the fate of his uncle Colonel Haughton before his eyes, thinks that it is not right to live alone, and that he will marry some time, but that the time has not yet arrived. So he applies himself steadily to art, and daily improves in it, and is as happy as a young man can be, who has an occupation that he loves, who is industrious as well as clever, and has no fear of the morrow.

LONDON.
PRINTED BY W. H. ALLEN AND CO., 13, WATERLOO PLACE.

www.ingramcontent.com/pod-product-compliance
Lightning Source LLC
Chambersburg PA
CBHW031340070726
47496CB00017B/1360